THEY RODE TO VICTORY

THEY RODE TO VICTORY

Christine
Pullein-Thompson

Cavalier Paperbacks

First published 1972 by William Collins Sons & Co Ltd

Copyright © Christine Pullein-Thompson 1972

This new edition published by Cavalier Paperbacks in 2001
Burnham House
Jarvis St
Upavon
Wilts SN9 6DU

www.cavalierpaperbacks.co.uk

The right of Christine Pullein-Thompson to be identified as
the author of this work has been asserted by her in
accordance with the Copyright, Designs and Patents Act
1988

ISBN 1-899470-90-5

Printed and bound in Great Britain by Cox & Wyman,
Reading, Berks

Chapter One

June was grooming Seagull. June was small and fair, and lived in one of the new houses only half a mile from the comprehensive school. She had three brothers and a sister, a mother who was always tired and a father who worked for the Council. And she had just been selected to represent the school in the area riding competition.

Won't Mum be excited? she thought. Angela says it's going to be on television and the school's going to have time off to watch. She imagined the whole school assembled, watching, and suddenly she was nervous. Supposing I forget the test? she thought, supposing I let the whole team down?

James had been selected too; he was a West Indian, whose father worked on the railways, and he had two sisters. He had never expected to be chosen. He had once ridden the serpentine with such concentration that he had developed cramp in both feet. But now that he had been selected, he couldn't stop singing.

Both June and James had been riding before the riding school had been moved to its new position, after they had fought a long battle to save it. James had ended up in hospital and June had become a heroine because her aged uncle had come to the rescue, suggesting that the Riding School became part of the new comprehensive school.

Gavin had also been chosen for the team. He was dark

haired with a large mouth and clumsy hands. He came from a broken home. He was fourteen and had no idea of what he wanted to do on leaving school. Angela called him a born rider, and he was completely fearless. But riding was the only thing he could do. His writing was no better than that of a nine-year-old and his reading consisted of nothing besides war comics.

Angela Manners ran the riding school. She was now established on the teaching staff of the comprehensive school. She was forty, slim with curly hair, and she lived only for her horses.

Naomi and Nancy were there too. They were twins with freckles; their father kept a pub near the town centre. They had been selected as reserve riders. "Though which we will have of you I really don't know; we'll have to toss up," Angela had said laughing.

Now the twins were taking Flotsam and Jetsam down to the big meadow, riding just with halters, and bareback.

"I wish Gavin had been left out," Naomi said. "He's such a bully. I'm sure I saw him slashing someone's duffle bag last week. He always carries a knife."

"He's the only rider of the right age," replied Nancy. "And Angela says it may be the making of him."

"Well, I hate him. I always have and always will. Why couldn't she have chosen one of us?"

"We can ride next year; we'll still be the right age, and the year after, but this is his last chance."

They had reached the meadow now. An autumn sun turned the dying grass gold. It was nearly November, almost the end of the Indian summer which seemed to have lasted forever. They took the halters off and watched the ponies roll.

6

"If only Fiona could ride Buccaneer," Naomi said. "She'd win hands down."

Fiona lived at The Manor. She kept her half-bred gelding at the riding school, appearing at odd weekends to ride him. She went to a private school and was just about to take her O levels.

"She's too old anyway," said Nancy. "She's sixteen in a few days."

The leaves were turning yellow and gold on trees that soon would be bare. "We had better hurry or we'll be late. And you know what Daddy said," cried Naomi.

"Yes. And we've got piles of homework."

It was always like that; the homework against the ponies. Because of it, all the children were supposed to be clear of the riding school by five-thirty.

Angela stood watching them. "Hurry," she shouted. "It's nearly twenty to six. I shall get the sack. You know what the Headmaster said."

"We only waited to watch them roll," said Naomi.

Everyone else had gone. The yard was swept, the forks, the skips and the brooms put away. The horses munched at haynets.

"I'm going home for tea. Want a lift?" asked Angela. She still lived in the lodge where the stables had been once. Now it was surrounded by new houses with wire fences, and shared gardens in front. It looked old and left behind, with its ivy-clad walls and Victorian Gothic roof. Its small garden was overgrown, but autumn roses were out above the gate.

"Are you ever going to move nearer the stables?" asked Naomi when Angela had stopped her old, battered car.

"I don't know. I love this place, and so do the dogs," Angela said. "They like the garden." She held the car door open. On the floor was a mixture of oats and hay seed, mud and dogs' hair, and it smelt of spilt hoof oil.

"Thanks a million," shouted the twins, getting out and walking towards the bus stop, which lay beyond the play ground and the houses, the blocks of flats and shopping centre, which had all sprung up in the last ten months.

June reached home. She rushed round to the back of the house, slamming the garden gate after her. Mum was ironing.

"Home at last. About time too. Your tea's been waiting for the last half hour," she said.

"I've been chosen," cried June. "I'm representing the school on Seagull. Everything's settled. In three weeks we compete against Sundean Girls' School."

"But that's a posh school," Mum said, putting down the iron. "There's a princess there."

Mum was pleased. June could see it on her face. "It's seven hundred pounds a year to go there," she said.

"It doesn't matter. All the better if we win," replied June, munching Swiss roll.

"Your Dad will be pleased," Mum said, "But what about the strike?"

"What strike?" asked June. "Is Dad coming out again then?"

"The teachers' strike. What about Mrs Manners? Will she strike? They are being ordered out next week you know."

June could fed a tiny prick of fear growing larger and larger as the words sank in. "She won't strike. She's not like that. She couldn't," said June, more to convince herself than anyone else. "Who would feed the horses?"

8

"She would, darling," said Mum, putting away the iron. "But she wouldn't teach. If she did, she would be a blackleg."

"It can't last long anyway," June said. "I mean there's the O levels soon. What about them?" But she wasn't happy any more. She paced up and down the kitchen thinking, if only Fiona was here. She would know what to do. She could talk to Angela, but I wouldn't know where to begin and James is no better, and Gavin wouldn't anyway. He would never do anything I suggested . . . he's a nut case really; he must be if he cuts up people's bags with knives .... And there's only three more weeks, she thought again, and remembered that Angela had promised to get the team off PE so that they would have more time to ride. I knew it was too good to come true, she thought, and now she was crying, on and on as though she would never stop.

"But it hasn't happened yet. Don't carry on so," said Mum. "They may never go on strike. The government may give in. They'll have to in the end . . . ."

"In the end, but not yet . . . only when it's too late," cried June, rushing from the room, throwing herself on her bed, thinking, I knew it was too good to come true. People like me don't ride in teams. We don't travel in horse boxes and ride dressage tests and jump in posh covered schools . . . we never have and we never will. We aren't meant to. I've always known deep down that it was too good to be true.

James still lived in a basement, but his father had been promised a new flat after Christmas, which wasn't far away. On his way home James stopped to read a newspaper placard which was beside an old man selling papers. He had only just learned to read so it took him a few minutes to understand the wording, which said: TEACHERS STRIKE NEXT WEEK UNLESS DEMANDS ARE MET. He had never considered Angela a teacher in the true sense of the word, and he thought, there'll be no school then. I'll be able to spend all my time at the riding school. I'll be able to practise and practise until I'm perfect. It'll be like the holidays. He gave a leap of joy and started to run. No school, he thought, hurray.

His Mum was out working on the buses, but his Dad (tall and rather frightening, and still in his cap and working clothes) was home pouring cold tea from his thermos into the sink, shouting at the other children for their bad manners.

"Sit down and have some tea," he said, "Your mother will be home in a few minutes. You've got hay in your hair, Jamie boy. You'd better get it off. We don't want hay in our tea."

James found a comb. "I've been chosen," he said. "I'm like the chosen few. I'm riding for the school."

"You must be dreaming," Dad said. "They'd never choose you."

"But they have. I was chosen today." James couldn't keep the pride out of his voice. "We're having extra time off to practise, that is, if the teachers don't strike. If they do, we'll have all the time in the world, won't we? I'm riding Flotsam. It's going to be televised. You can watch. And I'm not falling off this time, like I did when we marched on the Town Hall. I'm much better now. Angela says I shall be good enough for a jockey one day . . . she's certain."

He couldn't stop talking. He kept imagining himself

in a covered school. He might go first because he was the youngest, because he was only eleven. Flotsam would arch her neck, her mane plaited, her hoofs oiled. He would wear new riding clothes provided by the school, and Mum would be at home watching. It was like a miracle, like all his dreams coming true. She'll take time off from the buses, he thought. She'll watch and afterwards she'll know that I can really ride, that one day I really will be a jockey. And the neighbours will watch too - the whole street.

Gavin rode his bike slowly home. He lived with his mother and two younger brothers in a house where the town met the country. The town dumped its rubbish there; it stretched like a sea behind their house, and the rats invaded their larder at night unless they kept a bevy of cats. The house was empty when he reached it. His brothers were out on the rubbish dump searching for wheels and his mother was working a late shift at the factory. Gavin's father had left for good years ago when his two brothers were little more than babies. So there was no one to tell, nothing but the empty house, and the mewing cats waiting at the door.

If the teachers do go on strike, she will strike too, thought Gavin with anger mounting inside him. And it's my last chance, my only chance, as next year I'll be too old. I will have left school. He had known for some time that he would be chosen, for there was no one else of his age good enough. He had ridden a great deal when he was seven at his foster parents' farm. He had ridden a dappled grey called Periwinkle bareback across the Shropshire hills. Now he rode glued to the saddle; he had only to learn the aids from Angela. The farmer's wife had wanted to adopt him, but his mother had asked for him back. He remembered returning home. It had seemed the darkest day of his life. He had never got over the stay at the farm - it was the only time he had really been happy. But now there was no one to tell, no one to say, "What wonderful news!" to share his triumph with . . . just the empty house and the mewing cats.

I don't care, he thought, I'm tough. I can look after myself. If she strikes, I'm still going. Nothing is going to stop me, nothing, nothing on earth. I may not have a father at home, and we may live here, but I can still ride, and I'm going to . . . I'm going to show the whole school that I can ride . . . Snooty old Mr Heathers, wet-nosed Simpson, everyone. I'm going to have my name on the scroll of honour if it kills me. I'm going to be remembered and no one will ever be able to cock their nose at me again. He started to eat bread and margarine, staring out of the window at the rubbish dump, but not seeing it, seeing himself instead dressed immaculately riding flea-bitten Trooper, going forward to receive a cup beneath a spotlight, bowing his head, turning to acknowledge the cheers of the school. I can win if they'll just give me the chance, he thought.

Fiona was waiting in the school porch. She should have been inside. Matron had said so. "Stay well wrapped up, don't get cold. Chicken pox can be serious," she had said.

Fiona was in school uniform, clutching a suitcase. She could see her mother's car coming up the drive now. She ran out onto the gravel to meet it.

"I'm quite all right," she called. "I haven't even got a

12

temperature. Dr Nicols, the school doctor, says I can ride if I feel like it. She says it's a very mild sort of chicken pox this year."

Fiona was tall and dark with a nose which turned up at the end. She had spent yesterday in the school sanatorium at the top of the boarding house. Now she couldn't wait to get home.

"Is Buccaneer all right?" she asked when her suitcase was in the back of the car and she was beside her mother in the front.

"I expect so. Angela Manners hasn't said anything."

"I wish I could hunt," Fiona said. "I never have. How long is the quarantine for chicken pox? Matron wouldn't tell me."

"Until all the scabs have gone."

Matron had appeared by this time. "She needs to keep warm and she mustn't scratch," she said. "We don't want the scabs infected."

Another five minutes and they were through the town, gliding away into open country where the farmsteads huddled low and compact in the valleys and the villages were built round the manor house and the church.

"Has Alan got his horse yet?"

"Yes, or so I've heard. His father paid five hundred pounds for it."

"We'll be able to ride together then."

Fiona could see her own town in the distance now, and the nuclear power station beyond, like towers built of grey sand on the horizon.

"Dr Nicols says I can't hang about the tack room, or invite other children into Buccaneer's loose box when I'm inside; outside I'm not infectious." She wanted to sing. Three weeks or more stretched ahead, an unexpected holiday, three weeks for schooling Buccaneer, and riding through the woods over a carpet of fallen leaves. It was a bonus she had never expected.

"Your bed's made up if you want to get into it," said her mother, who had well-arranged grey hair, and wore a suit and pearls. "I've given you the spare bedroom's electric blanket."

"But I don't want to go to bed," shrieked Fiona. "I feel perfectly well. I'm going to the riding school as soon as we've had lunch. Have they chosen the team yet to represent the school? Is June in it?"

"I don't know. But you're not going there after lunch, not today. I'm sorry."

They had reached the Manor where they lived. It was old and gracious, peaceful and a little odd, standing as it was, surrounded by high blocks of flats and new houses. The house had beautiful sash windows, pillars round the front door, and a walled garden for which developers offered vast sums of money. There were seven bedrooms, an enormous kitchen, four reception rooms and two bathrooms.

"It's lovely to be home," said Fiona, getting out of the car. "I shall ring up Angela this evening. I must know who's in the team. And I want to know about Alan's horse. That's terribly important."

Alan had only just returned from his crammer when the telephone rang. He was trying to get a maths O level, so that he could enter the army at some later date. He was tall, dark-haired, and lived with his parents in a sumptuous modern house.

"Hullo," he said, his mind still on maths.

"It's Fiona. I've got chicken pox. What's your horse

14

like?" asked the voice at the other end.

"Fiona?" he said to gain time. "My horse? It's a mare. She's grey and she's called Fantasy, and she's got the most perfect temperament - nothing upsets her and she never hots up. She's done a bit of dressage and she's a fabulous jumper, with short cannon bones and fantastically marvellous hoofs."

He had always been able to make things sound wonderful, Fiona remembered. Probably the mare was quite ordinary, just a middle-aged grey with a splint or two.

He was still talking. "Are you very infectious?" he asked. "Do you know whether the team's been chosen yet?"

"No. I'm going to ring Angela later this evening," she replied, trying to imagine Alan riding a grey mare.

"Let me know what she says," replied Alan. "And hurry over tomorrow and look at Fantasy. She's going to compete against you all next year, so you may as well know what you're up against." He was laughing; suddenly he felt almost drunk with happiness. He saw himself riding cross-country on Fantasy, competing against Fiona on equal terms, performing a perfect dressage test, his photograph in *Horse and Hound*. He went to the window and looked out. But he didn't see any of it. He saw himself in the spring galloping across country on his grey mare, the wind in his face, the crowd on the hill cheering, the jump judges signalling him clear, his boots mud spattered and an uphill climb to the finish . . .

Chapter Two

THEY were all there the next morning, Fiona keeping away from the others, unable to stop whistling, as she imagined her friends at school, working or going for a walk in the park while she was grooming Buccaneer, impossibly free. Naomi and Nancy were grooming The Witch and Trooper while James was picking out Flotsam's hoofs. June was rolling up tail bandages in the tack room. She had told James about the strike.

"It may last for days or weeks," she had said.

"They may not pick on this school," replied James, with the voice of experience. "It may be just a go slow or a work to rule."

"If it's a work to rule, it will mean no extra practices in the evening so it comes to the same thing as far as the team goes," June said staring out into the sunlit yard. The yard was so new that the concrete was still coloured light grey and the surplus building materials still waited to be collected from behind the boxes. Gavin was riding into the yard now on his bike. He rode one handed, chewing gum.

"Any practice this morning?" he called. "Or is she on strike?"

"Who's *she?* Gosh, you're rude," replied Fiona, looking over Buccaneer's box door.

"She won't strike anyway," replied Alan. "She's not one of the blasted workers always wanting more. She'll carry on."

16

"That's what you think," replied Gavin getting off his bike. "But you don't know everything, even if you do speak posh. If they strike, she'll have to. She won't have any choice."

They could see Angela approaching now in her battered car, the dogs standing on the back seat looking out of the windows. She waved and called, "You're early. I've only just had breakfast. Are you here for a practice?"

"That's right, Miss," shouted Gavin. "That is, if you're not on strike."

"Not Miss. I hate being Miss. I'm not one anyway," said Angela getting out of the car. "As for the strike, I hope it won't happen."

James couldn't speak suddenly. He thought of days and days without any riding, of the competition being cancelled altogether. There would be nothing to do, no school, no riding, just a desert of boredom.

"You can't go on strike, Angela," he said. "What about the ponies? They need exercising and feeding."

"It's only a teaching strike," replied Angela.

"So we could still ride?" asked Gavin.

She shook her head and he could feel anger mounting inside him until he felt ready to burst out like a volcano, pouring insults on everyone. He wanted to shout, "You can't, you can't. I'm going to ride! I'm going to compete! You can't stop me. Nobody can."

Instead, he said, "You can still do it. You can teach us at night, Miss. Nobody need know. You must want us to win, and there's only two weeks left." It was far too controlled for his voice. It was like someone else speaking.

"I'm not discussing what hasn't happened yet," replied

17

Angela turning away. "It's a waste of breath."

"You don't understand," shouted Gavin. "I've never been chosen before for anything, not even the football team. And now you want to stop it."

"It's not me," Angela said wearily. "I don't want to strike."

"I've learnt the test; it took me hours, but I learnt it," Gavin said. "I know every word of it."

"So do I," said June. "But it isn't Angela's fault if we can't go; it's the educational people's for not paying teachers more."

"You've got another chance; but I shall have left school next year," replied Gavin bitterly. "Mum wants me earning good money. I shall be on a building site."

No one spoke. They were all suddenly sorry for Gavin. James imagined him carrying bricks in rubber boots turned down at the tops.

"You'll earn very good money, Gavin," he said. "You'll be able to pay for your rides."

"My Mum wants us to move somewhere decent," he said. "She wants my brothers to have a chance."

He was in his tunnel again, and there wasn't any light at the end. He felt like smashing his fist into someone's face. Instead he fetched a set of grooming tools from the tack room and started to groom Trooper. I'm not going to give in, he thought, I'm still going to practise whatever happens.

"I'm glad I'm not in the team," said Fiona. "It must be a terrible strain. I thought riding was meant to be fun but Gavin's making a toil out of a pleasure."

It was a phrase her mother used to her over and over again. "Don't make a toil out of a pleasure," she would say when Fiona was still boning her boots or cleaning

18

her tack at ten o'clock at night, or was setting her clock for four-thirty am on a show morning. And now she was using it herself.

The early sunlight was fading from the sky. They could all sense the rain which was coming.

"There's a meeting this afternoon. If there's a strike it will start on Tuesday. And we are one of the selected schools," Angela said.

"And you're shut on Mondays. Great, isn't it?" said Gavin sarcastically. "That gives us just today and tomorrow. And what about my brothers? What will they do while the schools are on strike? Bash each other up, I suppose, or get caught in the garbage crushers . . ."

Five minutes later they were in the covered school, Gavin on Trooper riding round at an extended walk, James on Flotsam, June on Seagull because Jetsam had the beginning of a girth gall. James was thinking, I'm not good enough . . . my reins are never the right length and when I canter, I look as though I'm swimming. June was wishing that Seagull would wake up. She sat very straight in the saddle looking between his two small grey ears and she thought, I wish Mum were here watching from the gallery. I wish she could see me now.

They rode the dressage test. James forgot the last bit, and stood in the centre downcast and trembling, fighting back tears, while Gavin said, "He'll forget it on the day. I know he will, Miss. Can't we have someone else? There must be someone."

"Not 'Miss' for the hundredth time," said Angela calmly. "Start from the beginning again, James, and keep calm."

"He's doing his best, Gavin," said June. "Why are you always so beastly?"

"He's so wet, replied Gavin. "I can't stand his eyes; they're always so sad." He started to walk Trooper up and down. "I'm going on practising," he told June. "And so are you and James, whatever happens."

"What do you mean?"

"What I say. We'll practise in here at night. We can block up the windows, and put the lights on, and not a word to anyone, or I'll smash your face in."

"But . . ." began June.

"No buts either. We won't be harming anyone. We'll be doing Angela a favour by exercising the ponies. We'll stop them getting laminitis."

"It's the wrong time of year for laminitis," replied June coldly, but she could feel a trickle of fear running through her body, and Gavin seemed to sense it, for he said, "I'll beat you up behind the building site, or one of your little brothers, and no one will know who's done it. And you needn't tell Fiona either. She would never understand."

James had ridden the test correctly and Angela was putting up some jumps, but June was not enjoying herself any more. She sat on Seagull praying that the strike would never come, that life would go on as it always had, because she imagined Gavin beating up her brothers, leaving them small and bleeding in the pools of water among the bricks.

"Your turn now. I've put the jumps down because you're on Seagull," said Angela. "Do cheer up. What's the matter? You look as though you've seen a ghost."

"Nothing. Nothing at all really." It was as though she could feel Gavin behind her all the time now, saying, "I'll beat you up." She hardly noticed the jumps.

20

"Wake him up. Use your legs," shouted Angela. But her legs seemed to have lost their strength.

"We won't be practising tomorrow," said Angela. "I'm sorry. There's a picnic ride organised, and I can't put it off."

James rode beside June. "What's the matter, June?" he asked. "You look awful."

"I can't tell you now, but you'll know soon enough," June answered.

Alan had arrived. He and Fiona were going to ride out together. When Gavin saw them mounting he felt a stab of envy run right through him. They can ride whatever happens, he thought. They've got everything . . . money, horses, nice houses, time. They can stay on at school. They'll always have everything, whatever happens . . .

"Did it go all right?" Fiona called, pulling up her girths.

"Except for James forgetting the test again," replied Gavin. "He forgets it every time. He can't read, that's the trouble."

"I can," shouted James. "I won the reading prize last term."

"I'm glad I'm not in the team," said Nancy. "It all seems so dreadfully unpleasant. I'm sure something awful is going to happen. I mean, really awful. It's as though there's murder in the air already."

"I'm sure too," replied Naomi. "Gavin hates James, and James is terrified of Gavin. I wish Angela would throw Gavin out of the team."

"She can't, because there isn't anyone else good enough of the right age."

"It will be James who gets hurt, he always does."

More pupils had arrived now. The yard was full of strange children who attended different schools and paid to ride at weekends. Gavin dismounted and handed Trooper to a girl in a crash cap, breeches and boots. He looked at Naomi and Nancy talking together and knew that they hated him, but it didn't matter. Nothing mattered now but the contest between his school and the girls' boarding school, only two weeks away. Rain was falling in a steady torrent from a slate-grey sky. He mounted his bike and rode away shouting over his shoulder, "I'll be back this evening to hear whether the strike's on."

The rain seeped through his old mackintosh. His gloves were woolly and full of holes. I'll lick James into shape. I'll make him learn the test, he thought, bent double over his handlebars. Angela's too soft with him. She always has been.

"I'm going home," said Nancy to Naomi. "Are you coming? It's going to rain all day and everyone's cross. June's even crying, goodness knows why. You would think she'd be pleased to be in the team."

"We'll just catch the bus if we run," said Naomi. "Come on."

They ran down the lane past the new comprehensive school, past Angela's lodge, and the blocks of flats to the bus stop.

"It's Gavin's fault. He's horrible to everyone," Nancy said.

June was going home too. She had no heart left for anything any more. Angela will hate me for ever if I ride without telling her, she thought. She will never forgive me; but what can I do? There's no way out. And she kept praying as she walked, "God, stop the strike. Don't let there be one, please." Then she thought, I never go to church, so why should He listen? Now she could see Rosie her youngest sister, waving to her through the garden fence and she started to run.

"Mum wants to go to the shops," shouted Rosie. "You've got to look after us. We've been waiting for ages. Did you have a nice ride? Did you fall off? Was James there?"

"Do stop asking questions," replied June crossly. "I rode Seagull and I *didn't* fall off and James *was* there." She pushed the front door open and shouted, "I'm back, Mum. You can go out," and all the time she was thinking, he's spoilt everything. I wish I had never been chosen for the team. I wish I were dead in hospital. I don't want anyone beaten up, not on my behalf and I don't want to ride without Angela's permission. I'm between the devil and the deep blue sea, she thought, and Gavin's the devil.

Fiona and Alan rode steadily through the beech woods. It was still raining but they hardly noticed it.

"There's a twenty mile ride next month," Alan said. "I got the schedule this morning. I'll let you see it if you like. I'm entering, of course." Fantasy was trotting steadily, beautifully balanced, her neck arched.

"Of course I shall go," Fiona replied. "I shall start getting Buccaneer into condition straight away. With luck, I shan't have to go back to school again this term, so I can spend all my time getting him fit."

"There's two different speeds. I'm hoping to manage nine miles an hour," Alan said.

"I shall too then," replied Fiona.

"Gosh, isn't life wonderful in spite of the rain," Alan said. "I never really thought I'd have a horse of my own and now I've got one, and I think she's got huge potential, don't you, Fiona? Don't you think she might be good enough for Badminton?"

"Possibly. I can't say really," replied Fiona. "I'm not expert enough."

"Wouldn't it be marvellous if we both rode there next year and were first and second?"

"And the Queen presented the rosettes," added Fiona. "Wake up. We're not good enough, not yet anyway."

"Not yet, but one day . . ." They were cantering now, side by side, their horses' strides matching, the damp fallen leaves muffling the sound of their hoofs, the branches above sheltering them from the rain. If only it could always be like this, thought Fiona, if everything could stay perfect with no more O levels or A levels, with nothing but riding through sunlit or rain-drenched woods. I could be happy for ever. But something will happen, sooner or later - it always does. Buccaneer will go lame, or Fantasy will get colic, and there won't be any Badminton for us.

"Guess how much Fantasy cost?" asked Alan. "Five hundred pounds, and Dad paid without a murmur. Isn't it fantastic? And he's always been so tight with money; I've never had as much pocket money as my friends; I've always felt like a poor relation."

They could see the stables now in the valley below, the sheer white outline of the covered school, with the orderly line of loose boxes, and the houses rising beyond, new and toy-like, like things put down to be taken up again and put away.

"Something awful is going to happen; I feel it in my bones," said Fiona, slowing Buccaneer, feeling him drop his nose and break into a walk. "It's in the air. Haven't you noticed? It's in the stable yard - a feeling of impending disaster, and there's hate too."

"It's Gavin's doing," replied Alan. "He's too ambitious He would have died if he hadn't been put in the team, and now he's there, he's become a maniac . . . Look, the rain's stopping. It's going to be a fine afternoon."

Chapter Three

IT was evening. They had all drifted back. The rain dripped off the overflowing gutters. It had soaked through Gavin's anorak, which had ceased being waterproof long before his mother had bought it at a jumble sale. Fiona had come back to look at Buccaneer. She was always afraid of something happening to him, but this evening he was calmly eating his hay, his large eyes contented, his short cannon bones clean and unmarked. Alan was grooming Fantasy. June and James were standing together waiting without speaking, their hair plastered to their heads with rain. Naomi and Nancy sat on upturned buckets in the tack room.

"If she goes on strike, it will give the ponies a rest," Naomi said.

"Exactly," agreed Nancy.

"The meeting must be over by now," Gavin said. "It's nearly six."

They had switched the lights on half an hour ago, when they had first started to arrive on foot and bicycle.

"It's not the end of the world if she does strike . . . Strikes don't last for ever," said Alan calmly.

"You're not in the team," replied Gavin. "So you wouldn't understand."

"Thank goodness."

"What do you mean by that?"

"Nothing."

They hated one another; it was an inescapable fact. It showed on their faces, and in the way they spoke to each other ...

"It's my big chance," Gavin said, "and I'm not going to miss it."

"She's coming," said June quietly. "Look!"

Angela's small car was splashing through the rain. She got out slowly and looked at them.

"I wish you hadn't come," she said. "It makes it so much worse. Now you won't even sleep peacefully."

"We wouldn't have anyway, Miss," replied Gavin. "I had to know." He knew now, by the look on her face and by what she had said. He felt numbed by the news.

"We go on strike tomorrow," Angela said. "We'll only keep the children at school who have no mother at home."

"Like me," said Gavin.

"No, you're old enough to look after yourself."

"What about the team? What about practising, Angela? What will happen?" asked James, his small face twisted with misery, his eyes growing larger and sadder.

"No practising."

"Couldn't the Head make an exception for us?" asked June.

Angela shook her head. "There are three football matches next week against other schools, and a hockey match. There's the exams as well. How can he make an exception for us and not the others?"

"How long will the strike last?" June asked.

"Goodness knows." Angela shrugged her shoulders. "I suggest you all go home now. It's past six. Don't any of you ever eat?"

27

"Not much, Miss," Gavin replied. "Mum never cooks except Sundays. You're not going to cancel the competition are you? Not altogether?"

"I hope not. I should spend your time learning the test. You'll hear when the strike's over on the television and radio."

She couldn't bear to look at their woebegone faces any more. "I can't help it," she said. "I can't be a blackleg."

And June and James understood. They knew about strikes. Their Dads had struck. June started to walk home. She felt limp and exhausted. She had been on edge for so long that now that she knew it was like a damp squib fizzling out. It didn't even hurt.

"Goodbye, Angela," James said. "I hope you'll rest while the strike is on."

"You can go riding, of course," said Gavin looking at Fiona and Alan. "You're privileged, ain't you?" He mounted his bike. He could feel red-hot anger seething in his head. He was as tense as a steel spring as he rode out of the yard on his bike after June and James, his fists clenched so tight on the handlebars that his knuckles were white.

"We are still going to practise," he said, catching up James. "I expect you at the stables tomorrow night at six. We will go through the test together in the tack room. That won't hurt anyone, will it?"

"Have you asked Angela?" James was wanting to run. He was scared, so scared that he felt cold all over.

"That isn't important. What's important is that we win."

He was so much bigger than James. "I'll bash you up if you don't come, understand?" he said.

"Yes, Gavin," James said. "I'll be there."

Gavin met June where the houses began. "We're meeting tomorrow night at the stables at six."

"Who's we?" asked June in a small scared voice, more to gain time than anything else.

"Me and James and you, mate," Gavin replied. "Six o'clock, now don't forget. We'll just run through the test."

"We're not riding then?" said June with hope in her voice. "Yes, all right, I'll be there." She was running now. She could see home already. It was a refuge, the lights welcoming her, the walls promising protection from Gavin.

"See you then," she shouted.

"Right you are. Bring your copy of the test," he shouted back. His tyres squelched through puddles. Angela will be grateful in the end. She'll be glad when we win, he thought. He imagined her saying, "Gavin saved the day. He got the team together. He trained June and James when the strike was on. We owe him everything." He saw Fiona and Alan clapping with everyone else. He ceased to notice the rain. He was warmed by a tremendous glow of happiness. We'll win, he thought. I'll teach James the test so well that he will never forget it as long as he lives.

The next day was Sunday. Church bells rang. Gavin stayed in bed until lunch time. Fiona and Alan schooled their horses and talked endlessly about the twenty-mile ride. They increased their horses' oats and worked out an exercise chart, sitting together in the tack room. Naomi and Nancy were taken to see an aunt at Newbury. June helped Mum turn out the upstairs bedrooms and thought incessantly about the evening, and listened

29

to the church bells and wished that she was religious, so that at least she could count on God's help. James played football with some other boys outside the basement where he lived. He imagined Gavin bashing him up and wondered whether his nose would be broken, or whether Gavin would punch him in the stomach. He felt hot and cold by turns as though he had a fever, and didn't eat much lunch. He spent the afternoon lying on his bed studying the dressage test he had to know by the evening.

> X Halt-Salute
> 2 Proceed at ordinary trot (rising)
> C Track right

But now he couldn't remember where the letters were in the arena, for he could only see Gavin coming towards him in his imagination, his big mouth smiling, his arms outstretched to grab him, and he couldn't scream. He was petrified like a rabbit when it sees a stoat. He shook himself and stood up. Halt at X, he thought. I'm all right with Angela, but, when I see Gavin, my mind goes blank.

It was evening at last - a raw, grey November evening with a mist lying on the meadows, and a dampness which ate into your bones.

"I've got to go out, Mum. Won't be long. I've just got to go through the test," James said. He had put on jeans and an anorak.

"But I thought Mrs Manners was on strike," his mother said.

"I'm going through it with Gavin. June's coming too."

He shut the door after him. Everything was grey outside, He started to run. The lights were out in Angela's house. Perhaps she's at the stables, he thought with hope rising inside him. If she's there, everything will be all right.

"Got to go. Mum," June said. "It's a practice."

"What, at this time?" cried her mother. "Who's bringing you back then? I don't want you coming home alone in the dark."

"Oh, Mum. It's not far. I'll be with the others anyway" . . . Five minutes later, she was at the stables. Gavin was waiting in the tack room with James. There was a sack hung over the window.

"We're okay. Angela's out," Gavin said. "Take a pew. We'll just run through the test."

He felt better now. His sense of frustration had gone. He wanted June and James to like him.

"It's easy really," he said. "Nothing to it."

James's hands were clasped together as though be was praying. There were rows of saddles on brackets, bridles, a shelf of medicines and liniments, boxes of leg bandages and a cupboard full of grooming tools. It had been like a second home to James for a long time; now suddenly everything was changed. He was ashamed to be there trespassing without Angela's permission. She had trusted him, and now he was betraying that trust. He felt cold all over and rather sick, while Gavin began reading the test through slowly, over-pronouncing each word as though he were reading to a very small child.

June was uneasy too. "I wish we weren't here," she said suddenly. "I thought Angela locked the tack room at night. How did you get in, Gavin?"

"I found the key. Come on, each of you recite it in turn; then we'll ride," he said.

"But I thought . ." began June.

"Recite, recite. Time is short," shouted Gavin.

Later they tacked up the ponies. June could hardly speak because she was crying into Seagull's mane. "They've been out today for a long ride. They should be resting," she said.

James couldn't get the bridle on to Flotsam. "You aren't trying," said Gavin, going to his assistance. "And do stop trembling. Nothing awful is going to happen; unless of course you tell Angela." He had unlocked the school earlier and covered the windows he could reach with sacking and horse rugs. He led the way in on Trooper.

"We'll just ride the first bit," he said, "finishing with the first serpentine." He felt as though he were part of Trooper. Bits of his life came back to him as he rode. He remembered saying goodbye to Periwinkle, wrapping his arms tighter and tighter round his neck, while his mother waited impatiently like a stranger. He had thought he would never ride again, but here he was riding round a covered school in charge of a team! He remembered the farm. The huge barn weathered by years, the sheep lambing in the spring, the view from his bedroom window and the farmer, Mr Hopkins, saying, "We'd like you to stay, Gavin. You're a boy after my own heart."

He remembered his own voice saying incredulously, "For ever?" And Mr. Hopkins had said, "Yes, for ever, son."

And then his mother had come for him. He hadn't thought back so far for a long time. It was like re-living

32

a dream. But he could still feel the anguish of leaving after all that time.

As he rode the serpentine he remembered bending Periwinkle between the trees in the orchard.

"That was super," cried June. She had forgotten that they were in the school without Angela's permission; suddenly nothing mattered but the test. She started to trot towards X while the others watched. She knew it by heart. She could have done it with her eyes shut. Seagull ran rather than trotted; he tossed his small grey head and bustled along without any cadence, but he was accurate.

"Thank you," said Gavin when she had finished. "It was pretty good. Now you, James."

James rode slowly and carefully; his serpentine was perfect. He forgot nothing except his fear. And then it was over and, as they rode to the stables, guilt returned. They put their mounts away, wiped the tack over, put out the lights, checked everything, locked up and started homewards. Gavin carried a big torch.

Angela's lights were still out when they passed by her house.

"We didn't do any harm, did we now?" Gavin asked. "Nothing Angela could complain about. We'll meet again tomorrow and do a bit more," he continued. "Same place, same time. Don't forget. Our team's *got* to win, and I'm here to see it does."

"Yes, Gavin," said James.

"I don't like it," June said when he had gone. "I think we should tell someone . . . someone like Fiona, someone older than us anyway. We can't keep on riding without Angela's permission."

"Yes, June," replied James, his teeth chattering.

"I'll call on her tomorrow morning, early, before she goes out. I hate going to her house because it's so posh. But we must do something, and I'm afraid to tell Angela."

Gavin was home now eating supper.

"You look happy," his mother said. "Had a good time?"

"Yes, thanks. I've been riding, practising. I'm going to be in the school team," he said. "Are you pleased?"

She nodded slowly and he thought, nobody's going to stop me this time. Not ever again. I'm old enough now to decide things for myself. Nobody's going to push me from place to place ever again.

"Wake me at seven, Mum please," June said. "I've got to see Fiona first thing."

Chapter Four

FIONA was making tea for her parents in the kitchen. It was a big room with an Aga cooker, an old-fashioned dresser with mugs banging on it, and a big scrubbed table in the middle.

She was still in her dressing-gown and bedroom slippers. Outside it was nearly light, with cobwebs, cold and transparent, hanging like muslin on the hedges, and the sun just appearing in the east while a wan moon still lingered in another corner of the sky. Her mother's dachshund, Siegfried, Sieg for short, was barking at the front door, and when she went to open it, expecting a parcel, she found June, small and cold, waiting outside.

"Hullo. Gosh, you're early," she said. "Come in. I'm just making tea in the kitchen."

June had never been inside the Manor before. She wiped her feet very carefully on the doormat and followed Fiona to the kitchen, admiring the racing prints on the hall walls as she passed, thinking that the house seemed to belong to another world, to the country rather than the town. "It's about Gavin," she said.

"Do you like tea? Sit down for goodness sake. I'm not much good in the morning, not till about ten," Fiona said. "But let fling. I'll do what I can."

She was pleased that June had come to her, though why she couldn't imagine. Angela seemed a much more obvious choice.

"I'll just take my parents' tea up, and the post if it's come; then we can have a nice cosy chat. Have you had breakfast?" she asked.

June shook her head. She reckoned that the kitchen was the size of her own whole downstairs put together. She could see Fiona's boots standing in a corner and *Horse and Hound* lay on top of some cookery books. She looked out of the window and saw box hedges, and a wall with peach trees growing by it, a huge gnarled apple tree and rows of some vegetable she couldn't even name.

Fiona came back, still in her dressing-gown. "Fire away," she said, offering June biscuits from a tin.

"It's Gavin," began June. "He's making us ride at night without Angela's permission." Suddenly she wished she hadn't said anything, because, now she had said it, there was no going back. "You know how crazy he is about the competition."

"But he can't - the place is locked, and supposing something happened? Supposing you fell off and hit your head, who would cope? Anyway you're probably riding all wrong," said Fiona, pacing the kitchen. "Is James riding too? How many times have you been riding there without permission?"

"Only once. But we're riding again this evening at six," replied June, staring miserably at the dresser. "We haven't done anything silly. He's been quite nice really for him; but I feel so guilty. I mean Angela's been so marvellous to me and James. She let us have free rides when we had no money, and now we're doing this behind her back. Oh why did the strike have to happen, why, why?" She was crying now. She couldn't stop. Fiona

36

looked embarrassed. She fetched a box of paper hand-kerchiefs and put them on the table. "Why did you ever agree?" she asked.

June started to explain right from the beginning. She knew that she was blackening Gavin's name forever; I'm telling tales, she thought, and Gavin's got nothing, not even a nice Mum. If he had a house like this, she thought, gazing round the kitchen, he might not mind so much.

"The wretch," cried Fiona when she had finished. "The miserable, ungrateful so and so - I'll tell Angela. She can tell the police."

"Oh no, don't do that, don't tell Angela," cried June, jumping to her feet. "He'll know it's me who's ratted then, and he'll hate me forever."

Fiona looked at her in surprise. "Gosh, you are scared," she said, munching a biscuit. "All right. I'll come myself this evening. I'll pretend I've just dropped in to look at Buccaneer; that won't throw any suspicion on you and I'll tell him what I think of him, the beast. I'll tell him that I'm fetching the police, and they'll send him to Borstal. That's what I'll say. That'll frighten him."

"But you won't send for the police, will you?" asked June. "Because I don't think that he's bad really. It's just that he cares so much."

"I think he's an absolute beast," said Fiona. "Look, yesterday the ponies were out most of the day on a ride, and then you go and school them in the evening. It's disgusting. You all ought to be taken up for cruelty to animals."

June stood up to go. "I've got to see James," she said.

"And I've got to ride Buccaneer. I'll just put the radio on. We might hear how the strike's going. It's just time for the news," replied Fiona.

The teachers were still demanding more money. "It goes on," said Fiona. "What a bore. But at least the ponies should be getting a rest."

She started to scratch her face and then remembered that she had chicken pox. "Leave at once. You shouldn't be here," she cried, rushing to open the front door. "I'm highly infectious. I've got chicken pox, now you'll have it, and your whole family."

"Just in time for the competition, I expect," said June gloomily.

The street lights had gone out. People were hurrying to work, newspapers sticking out of coat pockets. I wish I was going to school, thought June. There's nothing to do unless I go to the riding school, but I can't because I can't face Angela. I feel too guilty.

She ran to James's home and knocked on the door. The basement smelt damp and the radio was on full blast. James came to the door himself. "Hullo, June," he said, but he didn't ask her in. He stood looking rather frightened and as though he wished she hadn't come.

"I've seen Fiona. She's coming this evening to look at Buccaneer and she's going to catch us riding, and frighten Gavin."

"Won't she blame us too, June?" asked James after a short pause.

"No, I've told her everything."

"That's okay then," said James. "But won't Angela be cross with us?"

"She need never know. Fiona's just frightening Gavin."

"That's all right then."

38

They had to shout because of the radio. June could hear James's mother smacking a smaller child. "I'll be going then. See you this evening," she said, backing towards the basement steps.

The road above was full of children playing hopscotch.

"Why don't you play, June?" they cried. "Come on, be a sport."

"I've got to help Mum," June answered, walking home along the street, imagining the evening, Fiona arriving. But will she be able to stand up to Gavin? she wondered. Supposing he goes berserk?

The day dragged slowly on. In the afternoon rain started to fall in a steady torrent and the whole town seemed wrapped in grey dreariness, which fitted June's mood perfectly, for now whatever happened she was certain that she would come out worse than before.

"You're not going out in this," said her Mum when she put on her navy school mac.

"Not for long," replied June. "I'll soon be back . . . honest."

"Well, it's got to stop, my girl," replied Mum. "I'm not having you out at all hours in all weathers like this. It's got to stop."

"Yes, Mum," said June, putting on Wellington boots. "This will be the last time, I promise."

"You've promised before."

"This time I'm keeping it."

She had to bend her head against the falling rain. The morning seemed to belong to another life. Then she saw the lights of a bike coming towards her. "Come on, you're late. Everything's ready," said Gavin, with rain dripping off his hair, and running off his mackintosh like a flooding river.

"Is James there then?" asked June, starting to run, wondering whether Fiona had left the Manor yet, whether she was ruining the whole plan. "Our clock must be slow. It only said five-thirty when I left," she said. "Is anyone at the stables?"

"What do you mean, anyone? Only myself and James. Who else would there be on a night like this? Or haven't you noticed the rain?" Gavin inquired sarcastically. "By the way, we had better remember to rake the school tonight. We forgot yesterday and someone's been in and made it look lovely," he continued. "So they'll notice new hoofmarks on the peat."

They had reached the stables now. There were pools of water in the yard. Gavin had tacked Jetsam up for her. He was dark brown with black points, a small kind head, and small Welsh ears. He was nearly thirteen hands and he had been in the riding school so long that if Angela said, "Back," or "Turn on the forehand," he would do it before he was given the aids by his rider. Angela called him "the clockwork mouse."

James was already leading Flotsam into the covered school; the big doors were open, the dressage markers in place. There was no sign of Fiona yet - nothing but the big empty school waiting to receive them. They started to loosen up their ponies. Gavin shut the big doors. June kept looking over her shoulder. Any moment now, she thought, Fiona will come in and the row will begin. They couldn't hear the rain any more, only the thud of their ponies' hoofs going round and round on the peat.

"We'll practise changes of pace now," Gavin said. "If we keep riding the test they'll get fed up with it, and if

Jetsam learns it, he'll keep doing the movements too soon."

He was remembering the farm again. He had learned to speak properly there like he was speaking now. At home he spoke like his brothers and mother; but here at the riding school he always went back in time. He remembered feeding Periwinkle lumps of sugar by the back door. Why had the Hopkins fostered him? he wondered.

June was standing still now, her eyes fixed on the doors. Gavin saw that they were opening - someone was coming in! He felt frozen - for a terrible five seconds time seemed to stand still.

"I came to see Buccaneer and saw the lights on. What are you doing in here?" shouted Fiona. "Has Angela given you permission?"

"We are practising," replied Gavin, returning to life. "And you're not going to stop us. We're going to win. The strike isn't our fault." He was trying to control himself, trying not to shout, but his voice was growing louder just the same. Trooper's neck was arched in front of him, his beautiful grey neck which reminded him so often of Periwinkle. He had never been really happy since he left the farm and Periwinkle, not until now when he was riding in the school, pretending that Trooper was his. And now Fiona was trying to destroy everything.

"If you don't clear out this moment I'll fetch the police," she shouted. "Go on, scram!"

June and James were riding out into the yard already. Gavin couldn't speak; years of wanting things and not having them all seemed to crowd together in his mind. He rode out after the others without speaking, in a state

41

of white-hot anger. Then he turned to shout, "You don't know anything. You can ride whenever you like. You're privileged. You don't know anything, you ignorant fool." And Fiona's retort came back cool and clear, "Be gone in five minutes or I'll call the police from the tack room telephone."

He wanted to rip the telephone wire from the wall; instead he led Trooper to his box, rugged him up, bandaged his legs and put his tack away.

"I've got to go now, because I'm going to a party," said Fiona. "But leave at once and don't ever ride without Angela's permission again."

Someone ratted, thought Gavin . . . June I expect. He watched Fiona go without speaking, but his anger was still there. "I'm going to get even with you," he shouted. "You just wait . ."

"Turn all the lights off," shouted Fiona, "and clear off before I tell Angela *and* the police."

He wanted to kill her suddenly. But he knew now what he was going to do. He started to lock up. "You can go," he told June and James.

But they stayed on, knowing that he was going to do something dreadful yet unable to do anything about it. June couldn't stop shivering.

Gavin went to Buccaneer's box and undid the bolts.

"What are you doing?" shouted June. "He's nothing to do with you."

"Why should she ride when we can't? Why should *she* have everything?" Gavin shouted.

"Leave him alone, please," shouted James. "She's all right. Don't do anything to Buccaneer, please, Gavin, please."

But the anger was still there. He slapped Buccaneer's quarters. "Out," he shouted, "buzz off."

And now Buccaneer was in the yard, trotting away from them all towards the open gate.

"He'll get in the town, he'll be killed," shouted June. "You fool! How could you?"

But he turned away from the town towards the woods and suddenly was lost to sight, though they could hear his hoofbeats in the dark, thudding along the track, on and on like a beating drum, until the rain drowned them, and Gavin felt his anger ebb away, and he thought, oh God, what have I done?

Chapter Five

JAMES ran after Buccaneer. Though he couldn't see him anywhere, there seemed nothing else he could do. The rain stung his face and streamed off his hair. The woods were darker than anything he had ever known. Every sound and thought were drowned by the driving rain.

"He's clipped," sobbed June. "He'll die of pneumonia How could you, Gavin?"

He couldn't speak. All his temper had gone. "Why should she ride when we can't? It ain't fair," he said.

He sounded like a small, sullen boy. He wasn't even frightening any more.

If only it would stop raining, thought June. If only there was a ray of hope somewhere. But I can't stand here. I must do something.

"Why don't you tell Angela?" asked Gavin. "Tell her everything. I don't care. I don't care if I am sent away."

June started to run down the drive past the shut school. She kept running onto the verge by mistake, for she could see nothing besides the lights from houses in the distance, which seemed to beckon her on, to be saying, there's help here. But Angela's house was in darkness, though the dogs barked hysterically, nearly choking themselves with excitement, when she knocked at the door.

The rain had seeped through June's shoes; already

she was soaked to the skin. I'll have to tell Fiona, she thought, and started to run on towards the Manor, her heart thudding against her ribs.

There were lights on at the Manor. Fiona's mother opened the door. She looked at June with horror. "But you're soaked through, dear," she said. "What's happened? Come inside."

June couldn't speak for a moment; she had no breath left. "I must see Fiona," she gasped at last. "Where is she?"

"She's at Alan's house. Do you know where it is?"

June nodded.

"Must you go? You're so terribly wet." Fiona's mother was wearing scent and a long dress and violet-coloured shoes. She seemed to belong to another world, where the rent was always paid and nothing awful ever happened.

"Yes," said June, already running back down the short path to the gate. She knew Alan's house. It was long and low, with a large garden of grass and daffodils, a double garage, and two bathrooms, and lots of glass everywhere.

Mum had once said that it didn't look like a home, more like the monkey house at the zoo. Music came from it now and all the lights were on. They're dancing, thought June, and look at me! I'm nothing but a drowned rat. But Fiona must be told. It can't be left until tomorrow. She would never forgive me if I did that. The bell went ding-dong. June pulled it five times before anyone came; then it was Alan in a pink shirt and blue velvet trousers. He appeared horrified. He couldn't believe it was June. She looked small and drowned, like something floating on a pond.

"What is it?" he asked.

"It's Buccaneer. I must see Fiona at once."

"Can't Angela deal with it? I'm having a party."

"She isn't at home." June's teeth were chattering now. Her legs felt weak and she was wet to the marrow of her bones.

"Fiona," shouted Alan over the shoulder of his beautiful pink shirt. "You are wanted."

There were some old muskets hanging in the hall and modern pictures; the sitting room began just round the corner - there was no wall in between. People were dancing in a strange assortment of clothes. A boy in a frilly shirt was changing the records.

Fiona was wearing a red dress. "What's happened? Has Gavin gone mad?"

"No, not really." June could hardly force the words through her chattering teeth. "It's Buccaneer. He's gone."

"Gone!" cried Fiona.

"Galloping away into the woods, and James has gone after him, and it's pitch dark and pouring with rain. I came as fast as I could."

"It would happen tonight, of all nights," groaned Alan. "I've never had a real party before."

Fiona was struggling into a coat. She didn't speak; hundreds of images were rushing through her mind - Buccaneer hit by a lorry, Buccaneer lying on a road with his legs broken, Buccaneer dying of pneumonia, Buccaneer being destroyed by a vet.

"I'll get a torch. Do you want me to come?" asked Alan. "How did he get out? He's got two bolts on his door, one top and bottom."

She took the torch he offered and followed June.

"Was it Gavin? Did he do it out of spite? Because if it was, I'll tell the police. I'll have him put into prison for years."

She was running, though she knew there was now no hope of finding him till the morning. "I shall have to get out of these silly shoes," she said. "Which way did he go?"

"Into the woods. But he may come back. He may be back already, Fiona," said June hopefully. She felt better now that she wasn't alone any more. He may be whinnying to be let into his box, she thought. James may be with him. Everything may still be all right in the end.

"I'll have to change. You had better go home. You've done enough and your mother must be mad with worry. She'll be ringing up the police in a minute, reporting you missing. It's after eight o'clock."

June imagined Mum drawing back the sitting room curtains to look outside, saying, "Where's June then?" And Dad would be furious. "Why did you let her go out on a night like this?" he'd shout. "Where was the sense in it?"

"Yes, I'd better go," she said. "Good luck. I'll be at the stables in the morning, first thing."

Fiona let herself into the Manor. "He's gone. He's out, Mummy," she shouted.

"Who, darling? What's happened? June came here looking demented. She wouldn't stay long enough even to get dry, so I knew something had happened," her mother said in her calm voice, which never rose too high, or shouted. A voice of sanity.

"It's Buccaneer," shrieked Fiona, fighting back tears. "He's gone. Undo my zip, it's stuck in my hair. I can't

47

bear this silly dress a minute longer. He galloped away into the woods."

"Surely he will come back?"

"I don't know; anything could happen."

The dress was off at last. Fiona left it on the floor of the sitting room and ran upstairs to her bedroom to put on jeans and a thick pullover.

"How was the party? Was it fun?" asked her mother as she came downstairs again.

"The party? Oh Alan's you mean - all right. Have you seen my mac? And I must have a torch. Alan's is running out already." She wasn't going to cry but she kept swallowing tears.

"Don't be too long. If he's not at the stable, come straight back. We can always ring up the police," said her mother reasonably. "Someone is sure to get in touch with them sooner or later."

"If he isn't dead," cried Fiona, struggling into her mackintosh. "Completely squashed on the motorway."

"But how would he get there?"

"The woods lead there in the end, and he hates rain, he always has; it always makes him gallop." Fiona was really crying now. She pulled on Wellington boots. She seemed to have spent an age changing. "Where's the torch? Any torch, we must have a torch," she shrieked.

"In the cloakroom, darling. Shall I get it?" But Fiona was there already searching desperately for it.

Meanwhile the clock in the hall struck the half hour. June had reached home and appeared in the kitchen like a child pulled from a whirlpool, dripping wet and exhausted.

"I know I'm late. I didn't mean to be," she said. "But

Buccaneer is out and I had to tell Fiona."

Now she was in the warmth of the kitchen, with the clock ticking on the window ledge and the draining board piled with dirty crocks, the last two hours seemed like a terrifying nightmare. She thought, if only I could wake up and know that it never happened, or that James could knock on the door and say, "It's all right, Buccaneer is in his box. He came back - he's quite safe."

But life isn't like that, she thought, that's what people call paradise - a world where no one is ever ill or dies, where nothing ever goes wrong. "Get out of those wet things, girl," said her father. "Don't stand there dripping water on the floor. Who do you think is going to wipe it up?"

"I've kept your tea, darling. You look awful. Let me help you. You look half-drowned." Her Mum pulled off her shoes. The other children were still up watching the telly in the next room. June could hear them quarrelling, switching from one programme to another.

"They say the teachers are going back soon," said June's Mum. "So there'll be school again next week I expect."

But the strike didn't matter any more, not now, not with Buccaneer lost, and Gavin guilty of letting him out. June didn't mind if she never rode in another team her whole life long. "Fiona will never get another horse like Buccaneer," she said, pulling her jersey over her head. "He was lovely; so kind and calm. He was perfect. She always said so."

"Is he dead already then? For goodness sake stop carrying on so," exclaimed Mum. "He's not your horse. Anyway he may be as right as rain in the morning, eating grass."

49

Gavin had walked through the woods for what seemed hours, without seeing a sign of James or Buccaneer. He kept thinking over and over again, it's the end of everything, of trying to be like the Hopkins, the equal of other people like Alan and Fiona. He had killed all his ambitions in one blow. No one would want him at the riding school ever again. He could see the motorway now in the distance. The endless moving lights of cars, tens, hundreds, thousands of them; they were all going somewhere for something - going home perhaps. But he didn't even want to do that. He was sick of home, of his brothers, his mother, the mewing cats . . . everything. And it was still raining. He had fallen twice in the wood. His anorak was ripped, his jodhs covered with mud, and he would never have another pair. From this day forward he made the vow that he would never ride again. He would take a job and forget about horses, about Periwinkle and Trooper and all the happiness they had brought him. He might even go to prison. If Buccaneer died, Fiona would stop at nothing. But now in the wood, with the rain lashing and bending the trees, even prison held no horror for him, for nothing could ever punish him enough if Buccaneer died. He turned homewards at last, finding his way by instinct, wondering what his brothers were doing at home without him.

James was lost. He couldn't run any further. He had chased Buccaneer to the end of the wood and then lost him altogether. He had been walking in a circle for the last hour; always finishing up at the same tree. He sat under it at last, wondering whether he would die of exposure, and when his parents would start to look for him. He wondered, too, whether June had told Fiona yet about Buccaneer. He started to shiver, but at last

50

the rain stopped. He thought, if there were a moon I could find my way home. An owl hooted overhead and he found it the loneliest sound in the world. Where is Gavin? he wondered next and, what will Angela say when she's told what has happened? Most likely the whole competition will be cancelled. Gavin will have to give up riding; he may even be expelled from the school. Yet he rides beautifully. He is the only one of us who really seems to belong with his horse, to be part of him, like the statue Uncle George keeps on his mantelpiece.

He kept falling asleep, and then waking up when the branches of the oak moved, sending drips of water down his neck. When he moved his legs, they were stiff, and he realised how hungry he was. Mum must have his cooked tea waiting for him at home, and here he was sitting under a tree in a wood, completely lost, unable to see anything! Why did I follow Buccaneer? he wondered. Why didn't I stay behind like June? I always do the wrong thing. He wasn't frightened of the dark - he never had been, not like his little sister who had to have the light on in the passage until she fell asleep at night.

The sky was clearing. He could feel the shifting clouds even in the dark and he could hear all sorts of strange sounds, as though the whole wood was coming to life. It must be mice and voles and rabbits leaving their homes now the rain has stopped, he decided. And then he saw a light coming through the wood and heard a voice calling, "Buccaneer, come up . . ." It was Fiona, carrying a torch. She sounded weary and short of hope, as though she was sure already that Buccaneer had died.

James stood up. His legs would hardly hold him for a moment. They felt as though they needed oiling at the knees. The thought made him smile for a moment, be-

51

fore he called, "Hullo, I'm here. I'm lost, Fiona."

She shone the torch on him. "You chased him, didn't you? Don't you know it's the worst thing you can do to a loose horse? Hasn't anyone ever drummed it into your thick head?"

She sounded bitter. She hated him at that moment, more than Gavin, more than anyone. If he had left Buccaneer alone he would have come back. And James simply stood in the torch's orange beam of light looking like a whipped dog. "Say something," she shouted. "Say you're sorry."

"I am, of course I am, Fiona," he answered.

"And now I shall have to take you back; otherwise your parents will be going mad with worry. Oh gosh, I'm tired of you all. I wish that silly competition had never been invented."

"But what about Buccaneer, Fiona? I can find my own way back," said James in a plaintive voice.

"It looks like it, doesn't it?" replied Fiona sarcastically. "I suppose that's why you're sitting under a tree."

"If you just put me on the right path . . ."

"There isn't a right path. Anyway, what's the point of looking any more? I can see the motorway too. He's probably died there and been carried away hours ago ..." She was crying now, on and on as though she would never stop. "And all because of Gavin's beastly temper. It's all so futile, so unnecessary." She wasn't talking to James really, more to herself. "Come on, start walking. I want to ring up the police," she cried.

And Gavin's probably eating happily at this moment in his house by that awful dump, thought Fiona. He's probably thinking, I've got even with Fiona at last. She'll never ride in any more Horse Trials, or on the twenty-mile ride. I've cooked her goose - "Can't you walk any faster?" she said disagreeably to James.

"I'm sorry, Fiona," he said, starting to run. But now everything he did annoyed her. "Why are you so humble?" she asked. "You're like Uriah Heap."

"Who's he, Fiona?"

"A character in Dickens. Why do you always say my name every time you speak? It gets on my nerves."

The owl had returned. He flew low overhead crying, "Twitwit twi woo". The woods were suddenly sadder than Fiona could bear. I shall never love them again, she thought, not as I did, and she remembered cantering through them on Buccaneer, with Alan, side by side, shoulder to shoulder.

She started to run, struggling through the mud on the track, hearing James's plaintive cry of, "Wait, Fiona, wait," and not caring, not caring about anyone any more, hating the whole world because of Buccaneer. And now she could see the town in the distance - hundreds of lights, no thousands, and she remembered it as it had been just five or six years ago, small and old and beautiful, with not a new house to be seen; just the village shop, and the cottages, the church, and the Manor, Angela's lodge, and the stables. But suddenly the new houses had started to grow like a crop of weeds, the flats rising higher and higher as though trying to reach the sky, the houses clustered together with wire and concrete between them, like hideous toys. And then the riding school had had to move to make room for more houses. In one of them June lived, and didn't seem to mind.

They were nearly there now. The riding school was in darkness, Buccaneer's door still open.

"Go straight home," said Fiona, parting at the end of the drive. "And never chase a loose horse again, as long as you live." She was running again now, stifling her tears, thinking, perhaps the police have telephoned already; perhaps there was a pile-up on the motorway with him in the middle of it . . . But most of the motorway was fenced, she remembered. He would have to enter it by a side road, walk out of the wood, past a farm, down a concrete road and then on to the motorway and to his death. She wanted to scream suddenly, to lie on her bed and scream and scream. She ran up the garden path, pushed open the front door. "Any news?" she shrieked. "Have the police rung? Is he dead?"

Her father was in the hall wearing a suit with a clean white handkerchief in his breast pocket. He looked immaculate but then he always did. Fiona's parents were both like that - they never had a hair out of place; they never lost their tempers, nor wanted to throw things. They were sane and reliable, clear-headed and pleasant. It was impossible to argue with them, for they were always completely reasonable.

"What a way to come in," said her father now. "You would think the end of the world was about to arrive; that the atom bomb was imminent, that we were all about to be destroyed. In fact, you've simply lost your horse. Do try and have a sense of proportion, Fiona." He sounded bored, rather than angry.

"I know you don't care. You never have cared about Buccaneer," cried Fiona. "You've never been to see me ride him in anything, not even when I won the Horse Trials. There's no need to tell me."

Her mother was there now, standing in the hall, still wearing her violet-coloured shoes. "Fiona, go to your room and change," she said. "And don't ever let me hear you speak to your father like that again."

"I've got to ring up the police first," said Fiona, going into the sitting room, not caring that her boots left marks on the carpet, that her hands left a smear of mud on the telephone receiver.

"I've kept your dinner for you; there's prawn cocktail to start; you know you love that," her mother said.

The police had nothing to report. They promised to make enquiries. Fiona put down the receiver and took off her boots and carried them to the cloakroom. It was half-past nine. She knew she could do nothing else till the morning.

Her mother took her arm. "Just a little wash, then dinner and then to bed. Paul rang. He wanted to know whether you had gone to the party, and whether you felt like the cinema tomorrow."

"I shouldn't have gone to the party," Fiona said. "I've still got scabs. Look! And as for the cinema, no, not to-day, tomorrow or ever. I don't like Paul. He preaches, and horses give him asthma; and he's smug. He thinks girls should spend their time sewing buttons onto men's shirts. He makes me sick if you want to know. And if Buccaneer is dead, I shall go into mourning. I shan't go anywhere for a whole year."

Chapter Six

It was another day with the sun shining on the rain-drops left on the leaves from the night before. Gavin didn't wake till eleven. He found his mother putting clothes to soak downstairs, and the whole kitchen filled with steam, heaps of patched and torn jeans, dirty pants, darned jerseys, soiled handkerchiefs. His brothers were outside playing somewhere.

"The strike is over. I've just heard it on the radio," said his mother. "So you'll be at school the day after tomorrow."

"I don't know that I'm going back," replied Gavin. "I'm near enough leaving age, and a few weeks or months won't make no difference."

"Oh, yes it will," said his mother. "We'll have the in-spector round, and I'm not putting up with that, not again." For Gavin had absconded from school before. He had run away twice shortly after his mother had fetched him home from the Hopkins' farm to live with her for good. He had tried to make his way back there and been picked up by the police.

But this time it was different. He couldn't bear the thought of facing up to the others. And James could have told the headmaster or Fiona might have tel-ephoned the school and informed the secretary of his terrible behaviour. He didn't want to be called to the study, to be caned or told off by the headmaster. He felt

56

too old for the cane. He wanted to start work straight away; it would help him to forget the last week.

"If you feel like that, the butcher wants a lad to learn the trade," she said. "It's good money. Do you think you'd pass as fifteen?" His mother was putting on her coat.

"I don't want to cut up meat. I want to work in the open, on a building site or a farm," Gavin answered.

"You'd best go to the Labour Exchange then, love," his mother replied. "I'll look in the window as I go by. They put the jobs vacant on cards." She was smoking as usual; she never really stopped.

"Ta-ta," she said, slamming the back door after her.

Fiona had dreamed all night of Buccaneer; first he was galloping on and on into the distance; then he was at a sale with his ribs showing and his knees broken; but the last dream was the worst, for then he lay dead in a lorry, and, when Fiona saw him dead, she awakened with a scream - and could have sworn she heard hoofbeats going past her window in the dark. She looked out, but there was nothing there besides the light from the lamp at the corner. When she next wakened it was morning.

"You might have woken me up. Has anyone telephoned? Was there anything about an accident on the motorway in the paper?" she cried, dashing downstairs in her pyjamas.

Her mother was writing letters at her desk. Mrs Pinch, whom they called their daily help, was vacuum cleaning the stairs. Her father was just leaving for London. "Angela Manners rang. I said you would call her back. She wanted to tell you that Buccaneer was missing."

57

Her mother continued writing. The morning sun made a bar of dusty yellow across the sitting-room carpet.

"It's cold; where's your dressing gown?" she asked a moment later. Ignoring her mother, Fiona picked up the telephone and dialled Angela's number and, while she waited, she could feel her heart thudding against her ribs like the pendulum of a clock, but too fast, like a clock which is gaining time.

"It's Fiona here," she said. "Is that Angela? Has Buccaneer turned up? Is there any sign at all? I've overslept. I don't know why. I didn't mean to. I must have forgotten to set my clock."

But Angela had no news. "I've rung everyone I can think of," she said. "I'm terribly sorry. I just can't see how he got out. I always check all the bolts before I go home - top and bottom."

"I'll search on my bike. No news may be good news. It means he isn't dead on the motorway yet," Fiona replied. She felt a ray of hope coming back, for at least he seemed to have survived the night.

She didn't stop for breakfast. She struggled into jeans and a jersey, put on her anorak, filling the pockets with sugar, before fetching her bike from the garden shed and setting off for the woods. She took a different path than the one she had followed the night before. She pushed her bike in front of her, searching for hoofprints, re-living the dreams of the night without wanting to, hating Gavin and James with an almost unbelievable hatred.

James was still in bed. "It's time to get up, Jamie boy," said his mum for the third time. "What's the mat-

58

ter, are you sick? It's gone ten o'clock and you're still lying there. It's not like you, and that's the truth."

"I'm all right, just tired, Mum," he said. "I just don't want to face another day like yesterday."

"And what was wrong with yesterday?"

"Everything."

He remembered Fiona appearing with a torch. Her words had been full of hate. She was blaming him for something he had never done; for he had simply followed Buccaneer - never once had he chased him. It was one more injustice, and James had had enough injustices.

"Shouldn't you be down there at the stables? The teachers will be back tomorrow," said his mother.

Fiona hates me, decided James; everything I say annoys her. And now he didn't care about the team any more; for Gavin had spoilt everything. He wished he had never been chosen. This morning he didn't even want to be a jockey. He just wanted to stay safe in bed for ever.

But his mother was pulling back the bedclothes. "Come on, up with you," she said, tickling him under the arms. "Get up and go looking for that lost horse. A *friend in need is a friend indeed.*" He had told her about Buccaneer the night before, dripping rain onto the linoleum which covered the entire basement from end to end, trying not to give way to the sobs which wanted to shake his whole body.

"I was lost. I kept walking round and round," he had said. "And then she found me and was cross." And his mother had said, "Never mind, Jamie, you did your best; that's what counts."

And now the whole night seemed like one hideous

59

nightmare. As he got out of bed, he discovered that his knees were still stiff and his neck ached. I shall tell Angela that Gavin did it, he decided, struggling into socks. I hate Gavin.

June was at the stables already. She kept asking Angela questions. "If Buccaneer never comes back, what will Fiona do?" she asked and, "Supposing he's dead, run over, can she sue the man who ran into him?"

But Angela only said, "Search me," and "Ask her. I can't speak for Fiona," and went about her business, mucking out and grooming, with a grim expression on her face, as though she had guessed already that there was a villain somewhere responsible for the whole catastrophe. June wanted to tell her to say, "Gavin let him out last night out of spite, because we've been practising without asking you and I told Fiona who said she would tell you if we didn't stop, or send for the police." But she couldn't because it would 'be telling' and no one at school told about another to a teacher unless he or she were a sneak and June wasn't that. So she helped Angela, grooming Flotsam and Jetsam, emptying the wheelbarrow, sweeping the yard clean, and didn't say anything at all about the terrible happenings of the night before.

But they lay heavy on her heart all the time and she kept thinking over and over again, poor Fiona, what will she do if she never finds him? And she rolled the tail bandages the wrong way, forgot to put the grooming tools away, and was generally so incompetent that Angela became quite angry.

"For goodness sake!" she exclaimed. "As if things aren't bad enough without you behaving like a bull in a china shop."

A few minutes later June heard her ringing up the police, saying, "Surely you must have heard *something?*" in an unusually loud and impatient voice. "Well, are you doing anything about finding him? He's a valuable horse," she continued.

The sky was brighter by this time. The horses stayed in their boxes, bored and uneasy, and Angela returned to her cottage to make more inquiries, and to do her accounts.

June sat in Seagull's box chewing a piece of hay and thought, whatever happens, the next few days are going to be awful. Sooner or later Angela will be told about Gavin's behaviour and then the whole competition will be cancelled, and James and I will be in the doghouse, and Gavin will be expelled. If only I had stood up to Gavin in the beginning, if I had said, "I won't go down to the stables to practise anything whatever you say, even if you bash me up." Then all this might never have happened. She looked round the stables and knew she loved them, would always love them, and blamed herself for everything. I'm no good, she told Seagull. I've let everyone down. It's all my fault.

Fiona had abandoned her bicycle. Now she was through the wood staring down on the motorway. The cars moved like toys on a race track. The woods beyond were copper and gold. Fiona feasted her eyes on the view, imagining herself on Buccaneer standing here, feeling sorry for the people crammed in cars, feeling like a queen. Then she forced herself back to reality, turning away from the motorway to follow a path she had never noticed before, and for the first time she saw hoofmarks, large and round. She started to run. Her heart started to race, and she thought, it must lead somewhere, perhaps he's turned out in a field, as right as rain. The brambles which stretched across the path were wet, and soon Fiona's jeans were drenched as far as her knees. At intervals the path nearly petered out altogether. Around one corner there was a small clearing with two or three stunted apple trees, and wiry grass, and over everything a smell of thyme. There were horse droppings here and more hoofmarks and Fiona guessed that Buccaneer had stopped to graze, before moving on. The sun was coming up above the wood, making everything sparkle. It was one of those unbelievable autumn days already, when the flies emerge from hedges, the bees from their hives and suddenly it is like the coming of spring. Fiona continued to follow the path; she felt better now. She was ashamed that she had made such a fuss the night before and wished that she could behave more like her parents I'm so undignified and exaggerated, she thought, and remembered a school report which her house mistress had written two terms ago - *"Fiona must try to be less exaggerated and stop making mountains out of molehills"*.

Birds were singing in trees. A squirrel crossed the path in front of her, an aeroplane droned overhead. It was all so peaceful, so soothing after the last forty-eight hours - almost too good to be true. But now she could see a chimney stack and beyond, another clearing, with a gap in a hedge blocked by a wheelbarrow. She started to run, following the hoofmarks, which led to the wheelbarrow. She clambered over and found herself on a potato patch fenced by wire . . . Buccaneer raised his head and looked at her and whinnied. He was still in his jute night rug. It hung over one side soaking wet. He looked cold and miserable and quite unlike himself. Fiona ran towards him; she had forgotten to bring a halter or head collar, as she had never expected to find him. Now she put her arms round his neck. "How did you get here? Why didn't you come back, you old idiot?" she said. He nuzzled her hair and stood while she straightened his rug. Then she saw an old man was approaching from the bungalow. He walked with the help of a stick. His whole body was twisted out of shape; he couldn't even raise his head to look Fiona in the face.

"Is he yours then?" he asked. "He came last night. I was going to telephone the police, but it's such a long way to the kiosk. You can take him back through the wood, if it's the shortest way. No one will mind. I blocked the gap with the wheelbarrow to keep him in."

Fiona was speechless with joy. She could only manage to say, "Thank you so much. Can you lend me a bit of string, please?"

There was nothing but weeds on the potato patch and a few potatoes waiting to be dug. The whole place was falling into disrepair. The bungalow, which was mostly made of wood, needed painting, the wire fences sagged and the garden gate was half off its hinges.

"I'm all alone," said the old man, making his way slowly back towards the bungalow. "My wife died two years ago come Christmas . . . I'll get you a piece of cord out of the kitchen; you can make a halter with it. I hadn't anything for him to eat, though I threw out a few crusts of bread."

"We're going home," Fiona told Buccaneer, "and you can have a bran mash to warm you up, with oats and carrots in it, and a dry rug and lots of hay." The sun was shining down on him and she felt happy for the first time in hours. Everything is going to be all right after all, she thought.

The old man came back with the cord. She thanked him for everything. He removed the wheelbarrow from the gap in the hedge, though Fiona would rather have done it herself, for it took him ages. She was longing to be back at the stables, shouting, "Found!" and watching Angela's face break into a smile. She hurried Buccaneer through the wood. Soon he was sweating under the rug, so she took it off and carried it, worrying a little about his general appearance, for he was run up like a greyhound underneath, and he didn't seem to care much about anything, and walked as though in a dream.

"Wake up," she said. "I know you had a night out, but do cheer up." She passed her bike propped against a tree. The wood was drier now. In the distance hens were cackling. Presently they could see the stables in the valley below with the houses stretching beyond, row after row, and the skyscrapers looking like piles of children's bricks reaching towards the sky.

Fiona started to run, to shout and whistle and to call over and over again, "Found, I've found Buccaneer!" She stumbled over the rug and hit her elbow on a tree; then Buccaneer stepped on her heel, but none of it mattered - nothing mattered now that she had found him, now that everything was going to be all right. In her moment of triumph she even forgave Gavin.

She turned out of the wood and walked along the track which led to the riding school. She could see people waving from the yard and thought she heard someone shouting, "Hurray, hurray! Look, Fiona's found Buccaneer."

"I've got him," she shouted. "And he's all right."

He wouldn't trot, so she walked the last bit, down into the yard where June and James and Angela stood waiting like a reception committee.

"Where was he?" they shouted, and "Well done."

Alan appeared from the covered school on Fantasy. "You've got him then?" he asked.

Someone had mucked out his box. There was clean water waiting for him in the teak bucket, which Fiona had bought one Christmas out of the money her horsy aunt had sent. "I'll fill him a haynet," offered June.

"I'll get something to rub him down with, Fiona," offered James.

Angela just stood looking at him; then she felt his neck.

"Was he galloping when you found him?" she asked.

Fiona shook her head. She felt a sense of fear growing inside her.

"Did you gallop him home?"

"No."

"Then why is he sweating?" demanded Angela. "I'm going to get the thermometer."

She ran to the tack room, and Angela didn't often run. She came back with the thermometer. Fiona could feel a lump rising in her throat. "Perhaps it's just a chill," she said. "Or perhaps he was upset because he was lost. People do sweat when they're frightened, don't they?"

Angela nodded. "But he's not frightened now, and he's still sweating," she reasoned, taking the thermometer from under his tail.

Suddenly it was as though everyone had been frozen into statues. No one spoke or moved while Angela read the thermometer.

"No temperature," she said, "which is a pity. I'm going to ring the vet just the same, the best vet in England if I can get him. Let him have some hay, and someone put the kettle on for a mash, and look slippy."

Chapter Seven

The vet was a long time coming. No one went home. They stood about looking disconsolate, Fiona too frightened even to talk, with a sick feeling inside her growing tighter and tighter until she could have screamed; June thinking over and over again, I hate Gavin, it's all his doing, though deep down she was still blaming herself; James's large eyes sadder than they had ever been; Angela thinking, I know what he's got but I'm not telling anyone yet, not till I'm sure beyond all possible doubt. Alan tried desperately to cheer everyone up. It was his crammer's birthday, a yearly holiday which he had been looking forward to for weeks; now it was ruined. It seemed unfair that Buccaneer should be so ill, while Fantasy was as fit as a fiddle, leaning over the box door to watch everybody, her eyes alive and sparkling, the very picture of good health. The sun was shining over everything, over the boxes, and the horses' heads, and the trees in the field beyond. It was a summer's day in November, a reason for rejoicing, but because of Buccaneer they stood about like people at a funeral. And where is Gavin? wondered Alan. Surely he should be here too.

"Can't we have another vet, the usual one?" asked Fiona, "Must he be so terribly good? Isn't it just a matter of a jab of pencillin if he's got pneumonia?"

Angela didn't look at Fiona. "I don't think it will be quite as simple as that," she said.

"But what else can be wrong with him?" demanded Alan, wishing that somehow everything would suddenly be all right, so that the gloom would lift and he could enjoy the sunshine and his free time.

"I don't know, but I have my suspicions," replied Angela. "Now, why don't you all go home? It's lunch-time."

"Can't you telephone again?" asked Fiona. "Try and hurry him up. Buccaneer's sweating again and he isn't eating and I'm so frightened . . . Please."

Angela picked up the telephone receiver in the tack room. "They are trying to get Mr Tan Rivers on his car radio now," she said. They could hear someone talking at the other end, saying, "Calling DJ, calling DJ," then the same voice louder saying to Angela, "I'm sorry, I can't make contact with him."

Buccaneer was lying down now.

James and June went home slowly along the drive like broken people. "If only we had stopped Gavin," June said. "If only we had had more courage."

"He would have bashed us up, broken our teeth," James replied.

"I don't mind about my teeth. One can always have false ones, but there will never be another Buccaneer," replied June.

A haze lay over the streets. The basement smelt damp as James ran down the steps. There were sausages and mash for lunch.

"I shall be glad when you are back at school again, James," his mother said. "Then I can go back to a light lunch."

"I don't care what we have," replied James. "I'm not hungry anyway. Buccaneer's very ill; he's probably dying. Gavin let him out. I hate Gavin."

His mother put a plate of sausages and potato in front of him. "There's always two sides to a story, Jamie," she said. "Gavin's not had much of a life; his mother's no good, never has been. And he hasn't got a Dad."

June didn't want any lunch either. Her mother kept saying over and over again, "He'll get well again, darling, I promise. The vet will make him well; they've got wonderful drugs nowadays."

But June remembered the look on Angela's face. She had never seen it there before; she had looked frightened yet resigned all at the same time. And she hadn't wasted time, not a moment, and only the best vet in England would do. It all added up to one thing - Buccaneer was critically ill. It overshadowed everything. All the rights and wrongs of riding in the covered school at night were completely insignificant by comparison. Nothing is as awful as death, decided June, and she was suddenly certain that Buccaneer was going to die.

"I can't eat," she said, pushing away her plate. "I'm sorry, and I don't want any sweet either. I'm going back."

"I'll eat it," cried Rosie. "Pass it to me, Mum."

Outside the sunlight was still there. Passers-by had taken off their coats as though it was really summer, instead of a freak November day which June would never forget.

Mr Tan Rivers arrived in a large red car. Alan was still at the stables. He had brought sandwiches for lunch because his mother was spending the day with her sister.

Angela had just returned from lunch at the Lodge. Fiona had refused to go home and had shared Alan's lunch with him. Buccaneer was standing up again, sweating behind his ears. His hind legs weren't functioning properly and he kept licking his lips and chewing as though he had a nasty taste in his mouth and couldn't get rid of it.

Mr Tan Rivers was slim. He wore a cap, breeches and an anorak. He said, "Well, what have we here?" and stood looking at Buccaneer over the box door for at least five minutes before he went inside; and all that time Fiona was shaking with fear, terrified that he would say, "There's only one thing for him," and produce a humane killer.

James and June were both back by this time, standing behind Mr Tan Rivers, anxious to hear each word, yet terrified of what they might hear. Angela was grimly efficient.

"History, please," said Mr Tan Rivers, and because Fiona was suddenly unable to speak, Angela gave it.

"Eight years old," she said. "Out of Red Roses by Autumn Buck. A very fit and reliable horse, no previous illness of any description. Was let out last night and not found till this morning, and you know what a night it was. His rug was still on but soaked through. But he doesn't appear to have a temperature."

"And where was he found?" asked Mr Tan Rivers, in a bored voice as though he already knew the answer.

"On a potato patch," answered Fiona.

"Full of weeds I take it?"

Fiona nodded.

Mr Tan Rivers went to his car, returning with a length of tubing and a bottle. "Hold the bottle, will you?" he said. "I'm going to feed some glucose into his neck." No one spoke; nothing seemed to move until the glucose

70

had all gone from the bottle.

"Now for an injection of B 12 and Dexamethazone," he said, filling a syringe. "It's jaundice," he added slowly, "caused by eating ragwort."

Angela nodded, "thought so," she said. "I've only seen it once before, but you never forget."

"He'll need glucose in his water and a mash twice a day with about two pounds of black treacle in it, and plenty of attention to keep up his morale." He looked at his eyes. "He can still see a bit," he said.

"Is he going to die?" asked Fiona.

Mr Tan Rivers seemed to see her for the first time. "I hope not, but I can't be sure; one never can. But I'll do my best to save him."

And now Fiona understood why Buccaneer had to have the best vet in England.

"I'll be around tomorrow about eight if I can make it."

They watched him drive away. "He isn't going to die, Angela, is he?" asked June.

"I don't know. I lost one with it when I was a child. I shall never forget it," replied Angela.

"Supposing he goes blind?" asked Fiona with a choke in her voice, thinking, I can't bear it, not a minute longer.

"If he survives, his eyes will survive too," replied Angela. "Now go home all of you. He must have peace and quiet. Yes, you too, Fiona, you're so nervous you'll make him worse. Come back later when you've had a proper meal; bring him all his favourite tit-bits. Carrots, sugar, anything he likes . . . Now go all of you, scram!"

It was three o'clock. Fiona had rung home from the tack room exactly three hours ago, saying, "Keep my lunch. The vet must come soon."

She felt completely exhausted physically and mentally. Never had the way home seemed so long.

Lunch was waiting for her in the oven. "It's all dried up," her mother said. "Whatever made you so late? How's Buccaneer?"

"The vet was late," Fiona replied. "I had to wait. I had some of Alan's sandwiches."

The Lancashire hot-pot had stuck to the bottom of its dish. The carrots had turned black. The meat tasted like leather.

"What's wrong with him? A touch of bronchitis?" suggested Fiona's mother.

Fiona shook her head. "I think he's going to die," she said. "I feel it in my bones."

There was a short silence before her mother said, "And what does Angela think?"

"She's afraid too."

"But what's wrong with him?"

The tidiness of the house, the orderliness, made Fiona want to scream. Why should everything be so when Buccaneer's probably dying? she thought. She wanted to pull the mugs hanging on the dresser onto the floor and trample on them, for why should they be whole when Buccaneer was fighting for his life?

"He's probably eaten ragwort and going blind and dying," she shrieked. "You're always saying you get what you deserve from life, and now I'm getting what I deserve, though what wicked thing I've done I don't know." She was crying now. It was like a river bursting its banks; it brought a strange sort of exhausted relief.

"Any luck?" said Gavin's mother, coming home from

72

the day shift. "Well, did you go to the Labour Exchange?"

Gavin's mind had been far away. It was like coming back from a long journey. He gazed round the dingy room with surprise. "I was imagining myself riding for England," he said quietly.

"What an idea! Come down to earth for goodness sake," replied his mother crossly.

"I thought it was you who was going to look in the windows at the Labour Exchange," he said sullenly.

"Well, and so I did, but there wasn't anything besides apprentices wanted and skilled men."

"I could be an apprentice."

"And earn hardly anything? Don't make me laugh. You want a factory job, get picked up at the door, earn eighteen pounds a week from the word go."

"I'm not old enough," he replied. "And I've told you I want to work outside. Don't you ever listen?"

He felt sullen and unhappy. He was missing the riding school all the time now. It was like a dull ache inside him. He wanted to be with Trooper, to be leading the way round the school, to be practising the test. Angela would be teaching again tomorrow; but he couldn't be there, not after what he had done. And she would know by now. James would have sneaked - he was that sort of boy, or June . . . Yes, June would delight in telling Angela.

"I'm talking, don't you ever listen?" asked his mother angrily. "There's a job going in the fish and chip shop. How about it?"

"I want to be outside. I can't bear being inside four walls," he cried, storming out of the house, hating everyone, himself and his mother most of all.

And the sun still shone, that was the awful part, thought Fiona, returning to the stables after lunch; Buccaneer could be dying, but everything else went on as usual, or even better than usual. People were laughing and talking in the streets in the sunshine. Everyone was exclaiming the same thing, "What a day!" It was as though they had all put money on something at long odds and won.

And Fiona was creeping to the stables trying to hide her tear-stained face from them. It was horrible beyond words; she almost wished herself back at school - anything to escape the awfulness of the present. But Buccaneer appeared to be better. He had stopped sweating and eaten a large mash with a pound of black treacle in it. Fiona found Angela leaning over his loose box door.

"They have their ups and downs; he won't be really all right for at least a week," she said. "You mean he will be on the critical list?" asked Fiona with a shudder.

"More or less."

A week of uncertainty! It was almost more than she could bear. He had stopped sweating, but he wasn't looking over his door. He was standing in the middle of the box resting a leg. "I can groom him, can't I?" she asked.

"For a short time. He mustn't be disturbed too much."

Fiona gave him the lumps of sugar she had taken from the silver bowl in the pantry. Her mother was still quite calm about his illness. "Horses are very strong. Don't worry too much," she had told Fiona before dashing off to a meeting.

Now Fiona groomed Buccaneer with a body brush and thought, all this has happened because of Gavin, and Angela doesn't even know. She's probably blaming me in her mind for not fastening his door properly. He should be put in prison for years and years, she thought, if not for ever.

"I'm going back to where I found him," she told Angela. "Just to make sure it is ragwort he ate. It would be too awful if he was being treated for the wrong thing. Vets do make mistakes sometimes, don't they?"

"Not Mr Tan Rivers. Besides I've seen the same symptoms before," replied Angela.

But Fiona retraced her footsteps through the wood just the same, remembering how she had brought Buccaneer back to the stables full of triumph. As she walked she prayed, God make him well. I don't care about the long ride, or Horse Trials, just make him well again - and I won't even rat on Gavin. A breeze was drying the woods. They smelt lovely. The trunks of the trees stood straight and strong, tree after tree, raising bare branches to the November sky. And the sun was still shining. It seemed incredible that hours ago she was happy.

She reached the bungalow at last and climbed through the gap in the hedge. The old man was sitting on a seat but he didn't see her. She stood and stared at the potato patch and everywhere there was ragwort, ragged and withered. There was nothing else for him to eat, she thought, going back through the wood. Tears streamed down her face and fell on the fallen leaves.

Chapter Eight

THE next day the strike was over and Angela was teaching as usual. She had a special lesson arranged for the team, while the other children at school were doing PT or games. But there was no Gavin.

"We'll just have you two then," she said, looking at June and James. "Jetsam and Flotsam are ready. We'll run through the dressage and after that we'll spend the rest of the hour on the jumping. We've got an awful lot to catch up on."

James and June had changed mounts. James rode Jetsam who was brown like Flotsam, with a white pastern and a tiny white star. James pulled up his girths.

"What will we do if Gavin never turns up again, Angela?" he asked.

"Cancel the whole thing; there's no one else of fourteen who can ride," replied Angela. "I don't know what's happened to him. He must know we're practising to-day."

"Perhaps he's been run over," replied Fiona, who had been grooming Buccaneer, and putting her hand across his eye to see whether he would blink. But he didn't and she was filled with a dull ache of despair which wouldn't go away. He's going to be blind, she thought over and over again.

The others were going into the covered school now. Angela watched them while they rode the test.

"Well done!" she exclaimed when each of them had finished. "You have actually improved. Are you sure you haven't been practising?"

June blushed and buried her face in Flotsam's mane.

"We've been going through the test until we're sick, Angela," said James.

"Well, it's certainly had its good effect; there's nothing like work," replied Angela moving jumps, helped by Fiona. "And James is much better on Jetsam."

June looked at James. "Do you think she knows?"

He shook his head. "How can she?"

"But where's Gavin?"

"He's too scared to show his face. He must know Buccaneer's probably dying."

The jumps were ready. James refused three times at the hog's back. "Legs," shouted Angela. "Come on, James, ride. You are not made of cotton wool."

In the end she mounted Jetsam, who took her over the jump at once, looking as though butter wouldn't melt in his mouth. "Ride him as though you meant to go over it, as though your life depended on it. Hurry up. The hour's nearly up. It will be Chemistry in ten minutes," said Angela.

This time Jetsam jumped and carried on to do a clear round.

"That's better. But we are still six inches below the right height. You had better come round this evening for another practice. Come on, June, for goodness sake, don't just stand there. Warm him up," shouted Angela.

June went round flat out, bringing down the last jump.

"Do it again," shouted Angela, picking up poles. "And not so fast. Keep contact with his mouth."

"Just the last one again?" shouted June.

She took him back, slowed him down a little, then let him go, and they were over clear.

"Okay. Come again this evening directly after school. And we'll look for Gavin first. He must be at home," Angela said.

"Mr Tan Rivers is here," shouted Fiona. She was afraid to deal with Mr Tan Rivers alone. But he seemed to know that Buccaneer was hers. "How is he?" he asked. "Any improvement?"

"I don't know. I don't think he can see much," she said.

"His sight can come back. It will only be a temporary loss," he replied, following her to the loose box where Buccaneer stood with his head resting on the door, as though it would no longer stay up without support.

"Is he still getting glucose in his water?"

Angela had joined them now. "It seems a fairly typical case," she said. "Fiona's been back to the potato patch where she found him and there's lots of ragwort. I can't imagine how he got out - the whole thing's a bit of a mystery. I always bolt his door top and bottom, and I know I did that evening."

"There are plenty of hooligans about who would be delighted to open a few doors. I had my tyres let down in the town last week," replied Mr Tan Rivers, sticking a needle into Buccaneer's neck.

As he was leaving, he said, "I'll be back the day after tomorrow, unless you ring me. Keep up the glucose and black treacle."

Fiona ran after him, calling, "Do you think he's going to survive?" But Mr Tan Rivers would only say, "While there's life, there's hope."

"He doesn't care, does he?" she cried, standing in the yard staring after him. "If Buccaneer dies it doesn't matter to him, does it?"

"You can't expect him to feel like you do," replied Angela gently. "He sees sick horses all the time, day after day. If he was miserable about every sick horse he would be miserable all the time."

"Isn't there anything else we can do?" Fiona asked. "Anything at all?"

Angela shook her head. "Except go home for lunch. It's half-past twelve."

"Mummy's out at some meeting or luncheon," Fiona said. "I don't want to be by myself at home. I shall cry all the time."

"Have lunch with me then," replied Angela, opening her car door. "Hop in."

A middle-aged woman called Mrs Tibble came to clean Angela's cottage twice a week. She had just left when Angela and Fiona arrived and there was a smell of furniture polish in the hall and disinfectant in the kitchen. The furniture was shabby but comfortable. You couldn't help feeling at home; there was no feeling that you had to wipe your shoes half a dozen times before coming in, or mind your elbows on the chair covers. Copies of *Horse and Hound* lay in an untidy heap on the dining room table. Angela threw them onto a chair.

"Squash, cider or bitter lemon?" she offered.

"It'll only be scrambled eggs with chives on top, and cheese and fruit. I have my main meal in the evening," said Angela, bringing Fiona a glass of cider.

"Can I help?"

"Not now - with the washing up if you like after lunch. Read *Horse and Hound*."

Fiona nodded, but suddenly she felt too tired to do anything. Even to lift her hand was an effort. She was relaxing for the first time in forty-eight hours, and as she lay back in the chair she felt hope coming back. It was as though someone had injected warm blood into her veins. Then she realised that it was cider on an almost empty stomach and her mood changed abruptly. She imagined the knacker's lorry coming for Buccaneer's remains.

"I expect he will get better," said Angela, bringing lunch on a tray. "So *do* cheer up. It's silly to be miserable when there's still so much hope. And all horses die in the end of something or other, just as people do; it's life, you've got to face up to it sooner or later. I'm upset that he got out at all; someone must have let him out. Are you hiding anything?"

I can't say, decided Fiona, remembering her prayer in the wood, not unless he dies, and if that happens I shall tell everyone all there is to tell. "Oh yes, hundreds of things," she answered, trying to smile.

Later they went back to the stables together and looked at Buccaneer. "I wish I had a horsy mother," said Fiona. "Mummy and Daddy just don't understand. Daddy's always saying, 'Not riding again?' in a disparaging, disappointed way, as though it were a sin to ride. And Mummy isn't interested, though she pretends to be."

"My parents weren't horsy either," said Angela. "They wanted me to go abroad and learn French."

15 children from the third form rode during the afternoon. They were almost beginners so Fiona helped, putting their stirrups right, and leading those who couldn't make their ponies go round the covered school.

They wore jeans, crash caps and laced-up walking shoes, and their pockets were loaded with sugar lumps. After they had gone, school finished and June, James, Naomi and Nancy arrived in the yard, still in their school clothes.

"I'm going to Gavin's place. Does anyone know where it is?" asked Angela.

Fiona nodded.

"Okay, we'll go together. The rest of you tack up Flotsam, Jetsam and Trooper and don't do anything silly, please."

"We'll do the tack too, Angela," James said.

"And the boxes," shouted June.

"I hope we won't be as long as that," replied Angela, starting her car.

The rubbish dump was three miles away. It stretched across five acres. Gavin's house was by the road. It needed painting. Two thin tabby cats were licking themselves in the porch. The garden was overgrown; the gate hung from its hinges.

"What an awful place to live," exclaimed Angela.

There was a dreadful smell of rubbish and Fiona could have sworn she saw a rat peering at them from behind an overgrown privet hedge.

"Do we knock on the front door or the back?" asked Angela.

"I don't know."

They were too polite to hold their noses. "I suppose you get used to the smell with time," said Angela, banging on the front door. "But it must have been awful coming here from the farm," she continued. "You know he was fostered on a farm, and the people wanted to adopt him – they had him five years, but his mother came

81

and fetched him back. He learnt to ride on the farm. He told me about it once when he had hit his head and was slightly concussed. There was a pony he loved called Periwinkle. It must have been terrible for him to come back here. That's one of the reasons I so much wanted him in the team, because if someone does not get through to him now it will be too late. He'll have a chip on his shoulder for ever, and goodness knows where that will take him."

Bolts were being withdrawn now on the other side of the door. Then Gavin stood before them in jeans and a tatty T shirt. He started when he saw them.

"What do you want? How did you know I lived here? I suppose Fiona's told on me. Well, I don't care, not any more," he said. He felt humiliated. He had never wanted Angela to know where he lived.

But she only said, "We wondered why you weren't at school. We're having a practice; the strike's over. Are you coming?"

He had forgotten about the strike. It hadn't mattered for the last two days. "If you still want me," he replied.

"Of course we want you. There's only a few days left. Get changed, we'll wait in the car and hurry," cried Angela. He shut the door and bolted it. They could hear children's voices coming from the rubbish dump. Fiona felt sick; the whole place revolted her. As they reached the gate the rat she had seen before scurried across the road.

"Why should you tell on him?" asked Angela getting into the car.

"Search me." Fiona looked at the house and imagined Gavin a small, dark-haired boy cantering on a grey pony called Periwinkle. He was probably nice then, she thought. He would have been all right if he had stayed on the farm, and he might have become a great rider.

A few minutes later he was getting into the car, saying, "It's all right, I'll sit in the back," not looking at Fiona. He had obviously had a good wash in the sink for he smelt of kitchen soap. He talked in a humble voice, sounding like a reprieved prisoner. "It was nice of you to come, Miss," he said. "I wasn't expecting you, or I would have been ready."

"That's all right," said Angela easily. "I would have come before, but we've been so busy with Buccaneer ill."

"Ill?" exclaimed Gavin. "What happened then?"

"He got out and ate ragwort; he's on the critical list."

There was a short silence. Fiona stared out into the twilight.

Then Gavin asked in a breathless voice, "He's not going to die, is he?" It was more a plea than a question.

"We can't say yet," replied Angela. "It depends how much damage has been done to his liver."

The lights were on in the stables. Gavin's legs felt weak when he got out of the car; he didn't look at anyone, but went straight to Buccaneer's box. Naomi was inside giving him chopped carrot. "I think he can still see," she said. "I waved my handkerchief and he blinked, at least I think he did."

Gavin looked at Buccaneer and knew that he was probably doing to Fiona what was done to him, taking away Buccaneer from her just as he had been taken from Periwinkle. But *she will* be able to buy another horse, he reasoned - the thought didn't help him though for now he could only think, it's all my fault. If he dies I will have killed him.

"Come on," shouted Angela. "Get up on Trooper. The others are in the school already."

It seemed years since he had practised there with James and June without permission. It had been an idiotic thing to do; he saw that now. Fiona had been right to stop him. But he couldn't put the clock back, go back in time and leave Buccaneer alone in the box. I must have been insane to let him out, he thought, mounting Trooper, I am not fit to live.

He couldn't remember the test. But he jumped Trooper faultlessly. It was as though they belonged together. He went with him stride by stride; so that even Fiona said to Angela, "He's fabulous."

"I know. I knew it the first time I saw him ride," said Angela. "He's got enough nerve, enough sense of time ... everything."

"If only he was a nicer person," said Fiona.

Flotsam and Jetsam jumped clear rounds and Angela was elated. "If you go on like that you'll win," she said. "But Gavin must learn the test again, every bit. James must relax a little, and June must keep her hands still; a good rider hardly moves."

It was nearly dark. Fiona looked at Buccaneer, saw that his haynet and water bucket were full and went home.

Her parents were drinking sherry. "How's the horse?" they asked in unison. They were clean and scented and civilised, whereas she had hay in her hair and peat on her socks. "No better," she said. "I'm sure he's going blind."

"A blind horse is no good to anyone," replied her father. "Now listen to me, your mother and I have been having a little talk and we think it might be better to put him down and make a fresh start. We can go over to Ireland and pick you something really good. A really good five-year-old; I'm willing to let you have five or six hundred pounds."

"But I don't want another horse. I want Buccaneer," shouted Fiona. "And I'm not having him put down. Mr Tan Rivers says while there's life there's hope. How would you like to be put down when you were seriously ill if you still had a chance?" She knew she was shouting, and her parents hated raised voices, but she couldn't stop herself. "You wouldn't like it, so why should you do it to Buccaneer?"

"I'm not a horse," replied her father.

"No. But it's the same thing. Buccaneer was happy till this happened. He was on top of the world . . ." The peat from her socks had fallen on the carpet.

It's no good talking to her when she's like this," said her father. "Really, she's insane. Sometimes I wish we had never embarked on this horse business."

"Fiona darling," her mother said, "Do be reasonable. Dinner's ready and you haven't washed or changed. And now your scabs have gone, don't you think you ought to go back to school tomorrow?"

"School?" shouted Fiona. "But I can't, not till Buccaneer's better."

"Your house mistress rang up this afternoon. She says she wants you back as soon as possible; she says you're missing a lot of lessons and you'll suffer for it later on."

"Well, I'm not going back, not yet," said Fiona, leaving the room. "She can ring up as much as she likes."

Chapter Nine

NOTHING much happened the next day. There was only a week now until the competition. June and James and Gavin practised. Gavin hardly spoke to anyone. He kept his eyes on the ground unless he was riding and bolted whenever be saw Fiona approaching. Buccaneer seemed a little better; but it was too soon to be certain - he could have a relapse at any time during the next few days. Mr Tan Rivers said that if he survived another week he would live. He talked to Angela and Fiona for ages, telling them that he was treating another pony for the same thing, and that Buccaneer was in very good condition so he had an excellent chance. Alan was back at the crammer. But he came in the evening and schooled Fantasy. Afterwards he cornered Fiona in the tack room.

"Surely you're going to punish Gavin?" he said. "Haven't you told Angela yet? Honestly you are peculiar. He'll go and do it again. He must be taught a lesson, and if you won't tell, I will."

"No, don't," pleaded Fiona. "I've made a pact with myself and God too. If he lives I won't tell. I'll be so grateful."

"To whom?"

"To God or fate."

"You are peculiar. You never go to church and yet you have a pact with God. Honestly you're nuts." And

Fiona smiled at the way he looked at her, and then laughed. It was the first time she had laughed for three whole days. "Every night I dream that Buccaneer is going past my window," she said. "Isn't it fantastic? I get out of bed and run to the window and there's nothing there. Do you think I'm going mad?"

"Going?" laughed Alan. "You've been mad for years."

"Even if he does get well I shan't be able to go on the twenty-mile ride. Angela says it will be a month or two before he's back to normal," said Fiona. "But I don't mind." She felt much calmer now; it was as though all her emotions had exhausted themselves. "Mummy wants me to go back to school and Daddy wanted him put down."

"What maniacs! You can't possibly go back to school till he's well. Sometimes I think parents are impossible," Alan said. "Mine are so illogical."

The next day was the same. James and June and Gavin practised. Buccaneer seemed to have improved a little. Alan schooled Fantasy and during the night there was the first frost of winter. When Fiona returned home her mother said, "School tomorrow and no arguing. You'll fail all your exams if you miss any more lessons."

Fiona stood in the doorway with hayseeds on her jersey and said, "I won't go, unless you drag me there, but even then I shall escape and come back. I can't leave Buccaneer now not till he's out of danger and that's not till Wednesday. You can tell Miss Shane that my scabs have got infected and they can send me lessons. Please, Mummy. Don't be mean."

"It's all wrong," her mother answered. "It's giving in to you again. But all right, I'll try . . ."

Fiona flung her arms round her neck, and she thought, he's going to be all right. I can feel it in my bones.

And I like Alan, she thought a moment later. If he asked me to go to the cinema I would go with him. He's the only boy I really like. And he hasn't any spots, and he's amusing and he rides. Why can't Mummy and Daddy like him? Why are they always on about Paul? Then she thought, I feel much better. I don't think I shall hear hoofbeats going past in the dark again. I think I shall sleep all right tonight.

James was home too. He said, "There's only one more practice for the team this week, then one on Monday and none on Tuesday, because of the ponies getting stale." Suddenly he was filled with a great excitement.

"Your horoscope is good too, Jamie," said his Mum, who put great faith in the stars. "I looked it up in the magazine at the dentist's. It said, "A wonderful week. All your work pays off.""

James tucked into his tea. "And I think Buccaneer may be all right after all. He really does look better today. And as for Gavin, he goes around like a whipped dog, and none of us speak to him, only Angela, and she doesn't say much. Alan thinks we should tell, but Fiona won't; she says she's made a pact with God."

"Am I to get your clothes ready for next week?" June's Mum asked the moment she was indoors. "I want to know; your jodhpurs are split and your boots need soling."

"Yes, please, Mum. We're still going Wednesday. The ponies are jumping beautifully and Angela says Gavin should win the individual prize. The other school has two teams, the red and the blue, so there's plenty of competition. They ride all the time. They can keep their own ponies at school, and some of them are the Honourable this and that; Angela told us all about it today. She's told us not to be intimidated by them."

"Well, you won't beat them. You can't beat money, and they must have pots of it if they can send their daughters to that school," said Mum with a sniff.

"Oh, well, I don't care all that much," replied June. "I would rather we lost and Buccaneer got well."

"Will you be leaving very early Wednesday?" asked her Mum.

"I expect so. The test's in the morning; then we're provided with lunch, then there's the jumping."

"I can just see you having your dinner with all them Hons." said Mum, beginning to laugh. "Do they know James is West Indian?"

"I don't know. What difference does it make anyway, and what's so funny about us having dinner at the school? Honestly you are strange, Mum," June said.

"Everything's getting better," Naomi said to Nancy as they walked home.

"Gavin's not speaking, have you noticed?" Nancy asked. "It's most weird."

Tea was waiting for them in the sitting room behind the public bar. "Is the horse better?" asked their mother.

"A little," said Nancy. "By the way, we've asked to be allowed to go with the team next Wednesday. The headmaster is putting on a mini bus for supporters and Mums. Do you want to go?"

"Not unless you're riding."

"That's what we thought. Only they haven't got many Mums so far. Fiona's has a meeting and June's can't leave her children, and Gavin won't ask his ...

"Never mind," said their mother polishing her nails. "Perhaps next year you'll be in the team; then Dad and I will book seats in the bus. I don't know why you're not in it this year, instead of that terrible Gavin. You've ridden enough, goodness knows, and you're always at the stables."

"We are not fourteen," Naomi said.

That night Fiona had a nightmare; then she heard hoofbeats going past her window again, clip clop along the street outside. She leapt from her bed but as usual there was nothing there - just the pool of light from the street lamp and the silence of a town asleep. She couldn't go to sleep for hours after that, but lay imagining a hundred things going wrong. The church clock struck two, then three, then four. The first sign of dawn appeared in the sky. In the distance cocks started to crow. Fiona dressed and went outside. The moon was still up and everything looked sugared with frost; a dog was making his way home along the pavement. In one house a child was crying. Fiona stared at it all over the garden gate. Only six more days, she thought, and he may be out of danger. I can go back to school then and know that he's safe with Angela, that I needn't worry any more, and she wished that the days had gone already, instead of hanging over her like a sentence of hard labour. Finally she went back to bed and fell asleep, and didn't dream at all.

The ponies didn't go very well during the next practice, Gavin lacked the brilliance of the day before. He was living under an intolerable strain. Like Fiona he could no longer sleep at night and his mother kept on about a job. "You must know what you want to do," she said. "It's not as though you've got much in the way of brains and you can't afford to be fussy." And he could only reply, "I want to wait. Something may turn up. And I'm not fifteen yet. Can't you wait?"

"You will be fifteen in three weeks and I need the money," his mother said. "I need it for the others. I don't want to live in this pigsty all my life."

So he rode badly, and Trooper hit the wall and ran out at the triple.

"What's the matter with you?" shouted Angela. "You were all right yesterday. Have you lost the use of your legs?"

He was unable to reply because there was really nothing to say, unless he blamed his mother for her continual nagging, which sapped all his strength and resolution.

"There's only one more practice now, Gavin. I hope you're not going to let us down," said Angela when he had jumped the wall again. "I hope not, too, Miss."

"Not Miss. Please," replied Angela. "You're going to a very posh school next week. No one will call me Miss there. Call me Angela."

Gavin nodded miserably. He patted Trooper and said, "I'll do better on the day, I promise, Angela," and rode out of the school saying the test to himself over and over again.

They were all tense now and the ponies sensed it and played up. Yet Angela knew that without this tenseness they would never win. They had to be keyed up right to the last moment - they had to care enough to win.

James was so tense he forgot the test completely.

Angela felt on the verge of tears. "Begin at the beginning again," she said. "Halt at X."

"Yes, Angela. But what comes next?" demanded James.

June was better. She rode carefully, led off on the right leg, did an almost perfect serpentine, but when she jumped, Flotsam refused and she fell off. She lay on her stomach for ages groaning, while Angela said, "It's all right. You've just winded yourself. You will be okay in a minute."

"I'm sorry, I'm so sorry," she muttered.

"Better today than Wednesday," replied Angela, helping her to her feet. June saw stars and for a moment her legs would not hold her; then she was in the saddle again, picking up the reins.

"Start at the beginning again," shouted Angela.

It's cruelty to June, thought Naomi, for she and Nancy were there too, dressed in riding clothes, ready to take over if anyone hurt themselves really badly.

"If only she had broken her collar bone," said Nancy.

"Or if Gavin broke his neck, that would be much better," exclaimed Naomi laughing.

"Shut up, will you," said Fiona. "We don't want any broken bones; there's enough misery around already without that."

Lessons had arrived that morning from school - pages and pages of maths she couldn't understand, five grammar exercises on clauses and stresses and prefixes, and three chapters of geography. And she had to write an essay in French as well. And read what she could of

The Political History of England. She had gone to the town library and taken out a copy. Her mother had promised her until next Wednesday evening at home, and her father was furious. "I'm not paying bills for Fiona to stay here," he had shouted.

But Fiona and her mother had won, and Buccaneer seemed a little better. Alan had asked her to ride Fantasy.

"I've got so much prep I can't possibly ride her again this week," he had said.

So she had spent the afternoon riding through the woods, liking Fantasy immensely, though not as much as Buccaneer.

The practice was over now. Dusk had come to the town, mixing with the smoke from chimneys and the exhaust from cars.

"There's going to be a fog tonight," Angela said, leading the way back to the stables. "So don't hang about. Go straight home."

Buccaneer whinnied to Fiona. "He's better, but not out of danger yet," Angela said. "We mustn't relax our efforts for a moment."

The weekend was wet - rain fell in torrents from a leaden sky. Private pupils came and went. Trooper cast a shoe and the blacksmith came on Sunday to put it on again. Then on Monday Jetsam was lame. There was nothing to be seen, no swelling, no lump, no heat in his leg or hoof. It was a complete mystery.

"It would happen to James's pony," said Naomi at break. "It's just his luck."

"If only it could have been one of the riders," replied Nancy. "Then we would have had a chance to compete."

Angela was beside herself with worry. James was

almost in tears. He was given special time off from school and ran down to the stables to ride alone in the covered school.

"You'll have to have The Witch," Angela said. "There isn't anything else suitable."

"What about Seagull?" asked James hopefully.

"He's too small and he can't do an extended trot. Besides he hasn't any cadence," replied Angela.

The Witch was a bad-tempered, dark brown, almost black, mare of uncertain age. She bit the nearest thing when her girths were pulled up and had a nasty habit of stepping sideways onto your foot. She was fourteen one, without a speck of white anywhere. When she was in the right mood she would go beautifully; on other days she wouldn't jump at all. James rode her for an hour, looking small and frightened.

"If you're going to be a jockey, you'll have to ride much bigger ponies. In fact, you'll be riding horses," Angela told him.

But The Witch still felt big to James. "It's like driving a bus after a Mini," he confessed, trying to smile. "Her stride's so long after Jetsam's. It seems to last for ever."

The hour became an hour and a half, but James was managing her at last.

"Jolly good," shouted Angela. "That was a marvellous halt, absolutely first class." And James felt a glow of happiness which sent his spirits soaring. "She's super," he shouted.

In the evening he practised with the others. He rode a better test than June. And he jumped a clear round. Gavin was better too, though he still hardly spoke to anyone and was unable to look Angela in the eye.

94

Going home he wondered for the hundredth time why no one had ratted on him. He wasn't grateful, only puzzled. Had they kept silent for the sake of the team? He wasn't tolerant and he hated charity. I'm in their debt and I hate it, he thought. I'll ask them tomorrow why they haven't said anything; there must be a reason.

The next day was Tuesday. They cleaned their tack that evening in preparation for the event. Fiona was to travel with Angela in the cab beside the driver. The riders were going in the groom compartment, and everyone else was going in the minibus, supervised by prefects and the assistant games mistress. Her name was Miss Horsefall, and she had huge red knees and very short fair hair.

All the ponies were being ridden in eggbut snaffles. The Witch and Trooper wore drop nosebands as well. Mr Tan Rivers had been to see Buccaneer on Monday and announced him better, though still in danger.

"He's still stiff behind," he had said, "and his eyes aren't right yet."

Fiona had done all her homework, sitting at the dining room table all morning. She knew her maths were wrong but there was nothing else she could do about them. Like Alan she was simply no good at the subject. Her mother had helped her with the essay. But she had stuck in the prefixes. Her suitcase was packed ready for her return to school, her shoes cleaned.

Angela had gone home for tea. There were only Naomi and Nancy, James, June, Fiona and Gavin in the tack room.

"Why didn't you tell on me?" asked Gavin suddenly. "It isn't natural that you shouldn't. Why didn't you?"

"I don't know," replied James, staring at the floor.

"I didn't want to be bashed up," answered June. "You threatened us, remember? Or is your memory so short?"

It was funny; she had been so frightened of him, but she wasn't any more, not since the evening when he had let Buccaneer out. He reminded her of her younger brother. He got in rages too and threw himself on the floor and screamed and threw his toys at Mum. And then the mood would pass and he would be nice again. Mum called it his "temper tantrums".

"What about you, Fiona?" asked Gavin without looking at her.

Fiona took some time to answer. She didn't want to tell him about her prayer in the wood, for they might laugh at her, and yet that was the real reason, the overpowering one - what she called her 'pact with God'. But there was another one too. It was what her mother called 'not crying over spilt milk'. Blaming Gavin wouldn't make Buccaneer well again, only Mr Tan Rivers and luck, and perhaps God, could do that.

"There didn't seem any point," Fiona replied, "I figured you must be haunted by remorse anyway, and telling anyone wouldn't make Buccaneer well again, would it?"

"Didn't you want your revenge?"

She shook her head. "I'm too miserable to think of revenge."

She left the tack room to look at Buccaneer. He was eating his hay, resting one hind leg. He was thinner, and his skin didn't ripple, nor did his coat shine like Fantasy's, But he was still alive and that was something.

In the tack room Naomi said, "So it was you, Gavin. You let him out. You absolute beast. First you slash people's bags at school, then you let Buccaneer out."

"Beast," echoed Nancy.

Once he would have flown into a rage at such an insult. He would have shouted, "Shut up, you little squirt, before I bash your face in," and they would have run screaming across the playground.

But now he stood up and looked at Trooper's tack, which gleamed and shone like silver and rich mahogany and said, "I'm going home. Goodnight all. See you tomorrow at eight."

He stepped outside and Fiona said from the dusk of the yard, "Angela says I can plait Trooper's mane so you needn't come too early."

And he said, "Thank you, I can't plait to save my life." His bike had no light, so he had to lead it home, but it didn't matter, because there was only the night to be got through now before tomorrow - tomorrow the greatest day of his life.

Chapter Ten

THERE was a frost outside when June wakened. It had frosted the window panes, turned the rooftops white and tinselled the trees.

"It's today," she cried, rushing downstairs. "What's the time? Have I overslept?"

Her mother was cooking bacon in the kitchen. "It's ten to seven," she answered. "I was just about to call you. Your Dad's shaving in the bathroom, so you'll have to wait a minute. Your jodhpurs are clean on the chair in your bedroom, and I put out a clean white shirt for you and a hanky."

"You're an angel. And I cleaned my boots last night; but I shall take them all in the carrier bag. I'm going in jeans," said June, disappearing upstairs.

Half a mile away James was feeling sick with excitement. He was dressed in his riding clothes already, eating breakfast, thinking, supposing I forget the test? He had a pain in his stomach and a funny feeling in his head. "I shall be watching on telly, Jamie, I won't forget. The supervisor changed my shift for me. He was real nice about it. Have you seen it in the *Radio Times?* East Hanley Comprehensive School rides against Sundean Girls' School at 2 pm. BBC 1. The dressage is being recorded and shown at the same time."

"I wish I had never been chosen," replied James, pushing his breakfast away from him. "It's too much of a responsibility."

"It's an honour, you mean," said his mother.

Naomi and Nancy had to go to school as usual. "It isn't fair," they said. "Why can't we get the ponies ready too? We are the reserve riders."

They would be missing part of the dressage as the minibus wasn't scheduled to leave before eleven. They would have to attend assembly and sit through a double period of maths.

Gavin wakened when the bantam cock started to crow outside his window. It was a new pet for his youngest brother David, and had only arrived with two hens the evening before.

It's today, thought Gavin, and knew it was still early because there was no traffic travelling along the road outside. He shared a room with his brothers, which looked out on the rubbish dump and the woods beyond. There were lakes among the rubbish and sometimes wild ducks came and settled there; and small, round water hens. Today everything was covered with frost so that even the rubbish had its own strange beauty.

He dressed quickly in his best riding clothes. His hair nearly reached the collar of his shirt. He scrubbed his hands at the kitchen sink, and cleaned his nails with a match which he sharpened to a point with his penknife. His mother wouldn't be up for some time yet, so he made himself a pot of tea, and cut himself a slice of bread. He ate and drank standing up in the small, dingy kitchen and thought, I bet James lets us down or June refuses. But I can still win the individual. I can still bring a rosette home, my first, at just on fifteen. Oh well, better late than never and it will be something to hang above my bed. He wakened his brothers before he left, gliding away on his bike through the still half asleep town.

Fiona ate a leisurely breakfast in the kitchen. She thought, it's a nice day for them; it's going to be fine. Her mother appeared in a velvet dressing gown. "Why so early? You're not riding. And do remember that you are going back to school today. You have to be back there by eight-thirty at the very latest."

"I know," replied Fiona in a bored voice. "I shall be back in time, never fear."

The air was crisp with frost when she stepped outside. The moon shone down on her from a blue-black sky. A cat stalked along the street, and a paper boy had just started on his round. It was all so gloriously silent and secret without a car in sight, nor a bus, nor a lorry. If only it would always be like this, thought Fiona, it would be sheer heaven. She had put thread and scissors and a comb in her pocket. I hope James doesn't make a mistake, she thought. I don't mind about Gavin. It might do him good. But James has taken enough knockings one way or another. She could see the stables now, compact and beautiful in the moonlight, and Angela's Gothic lodge like something from a fairy tale, and the tall trees on the drive all white with frost, the puddles iced over, the mud rock hard. She was running now, singing under her breath, thinking, I wish I didn't have to go back to school tonight, imagining the town owls hooting at night, the curious smell of school passages. I bet someone's bagged my bed, she thought. I bet I have to have the bed by the door.

Angela was just arriving. She started by filling up water buckets and then by distributing feeds. At first she didn't notice that anything was wrong with Buccaneer. Then she saw that he didn't want to move and realising that he was lame, she ran into the tack room to telephone the vet.

So Fiona was met by her worried face. "He's not so good this morning," she said. "I've telephoned Mr Tan Rivers. He's at Newmarket and won't be back till noon. Do you want me to stay?"

"But it's only twenty-past seven. He can't be gone already," cried Fiona.

"But he has. He left at five," replied Angela.

"But how can we wait till noon?" cried Fiona, going to Buccaneer's box.

"He's not dying. It may be nothing much - they have their ups and downs," said Angela.

"I can't go with you then," said Fiona. "You can't stay. You must go."

"Yes, I'm afraid I must."

The others had arrived by now. The yard was full of chatter. "Throw me a curry comb," shouted June.

"I hardly slept at all, and I've got butterflies in my stomach," announced James.

Fiona felt out of it all. She sat on a bucket staring at Buccaneer. What can it be now? she thought. He seemed so much better yesterday. Gavin looked over the door. "I'm sorry," he said. "I am really." She made no reply, for now she was hating him again. He was riding, but she no longer had anything to ride; it was almost more than she could bear.

Angela plaited all three ponies; she lost two needles and worried incessantly about Buccaneer, while James groomed The Witch until her coat shone like dark patent leather. Daylight came at last with clouds like beaten egg white in a blue sky.

"He's eating all right," said Fiona, leaving Buccaneer's

box. "Do you want any help?" She felt limp and lethargic; she had been ready to spend the whole day helping at the competition and now she had to spend the day alone waiting for Mr Tan Rivers.

June was changing now in the tack room. She had put her hair in a pony tail, and somehow her mother had found some money for a new crash cap. Gavin was oiling the ponies' hoofs. His dark hair showed off the whiteness of his shirt. He had never looked so clean before. Suddenly on the stroke of nine, the cry went up, "Horsebox!"

Angela had changed by this time and Fiona was finishing the mucking out. The sun was shining on gleaming ponies, polished jodhpur boots and head collars. Every pony wore a tail and leg bandages, and had seven plaits including his forelock. Trooper's tail had been rinsed in Reckitt's blue.

The burly horsebox driver with tattooed arms and receding hair, asked, "Who goes first?"

This is it, thought Gavin. Everything begins here.

"Trooper's the old hand. He always boxes," replied Angela taking his head collar rope from Gavin.

Five minutes later they were all in, the ramp was thrown up, the screws turned.

"Good luck - bring back lots of rosettes," shouted Fiona.

"Best of luck with Buccaneer," replied June. "I wish you were coming too . . . I wish Buccaneer was all right . . . I wish . . ." Her voice was drowned by the engine starting. Gavin was in front with Angela and the driver. He had wanted it that way and June and James were glad. "Now we can chatter as much as we like," said June.

102

"Poor Fiona," replied James. "I do hope Buccaneer is all right. I do hope he isn't going to die."

"Oh shut up or I'll cry," replied June. "Have you got the test? Let's go through it together, just once more."

The girls' school had enormous grounds with five hard tennis courts and a swimming pool. The house was Georgian, but had been built on to, and more buildings occupied the grounds - modern concrete buildings with huge windows, the largest of which was the indoor riding school. When James saw the school he started to feel sick. The horsebox turned through pillared gates: the drive was long and impressive with girls walking along it in dark-green tunics and blazers. From somewhere drifted the sound of singing. A breeze blew through the trees in the parkland surrounding the school. There was a ha-ha and statues, and a balustrade.

"I know I'm going to fall off," said June. "I feel it in my bones, and Gavin will be horrid about it. He'll keep on and on at me, saying it was all my fault, that if it wasn't for me, we'd have won."

James knew how she felt. He asked himself, why did I agree to come? Why didn't I refuse, say to Angela, I can't, I'm going somewhere else? Someone else could have come instead.

Gavin wasn't speaking. He couldn't take his eyes off the splendour of the place. If I could live here I wouldn't want anything else; even success wouldn't matter, he thought. But they're 'the haves,' and I'm 'the have nots', he decided.

The horsebox had stopped. "Well, here we are," announced Angela.

They were in a stable yard with a clock tower and an arch, and rooms above the loose boxes. The ground was paved with Staffordshire brick. It made their own yard seem like a council house compared to a millionaire's residence.

A crowd of girls awaited them dressed in breeches and boots, their crash caps tipped forward over their noses, which made Gavin think, 'pack of snobs'.

They saluted politely. "Will you park over here?" one of them said in a drawling voice, which Gavin was already imitating in his mind. Well-bred horses and ponies looked over loose box doors. A girl in jeans was carrying a skip.

"It's twenty to eleven. We've just made it," said Angela. They unboxed the ponies while the girls watched, before they went off to lead out their own mounts which were clipped, with their manes and tails beautifully pulled. The girl in jeans stripped off rugs and bandages, pulled up girths and helped with stirrups.

James's legs would hardly work and he was shaking all over.

"For goodness sake," snapped Angela, "you can't be that scared." And suddenly they knew that she was overawed too.

"We shouldn't have much trouble licking them," one of the girls said.

June wished that there was a band to break into music; anything to take her mind off what was about to happen.

Angela held her stirrup. "You can get up now," she said.

There were some teachers waiting for them outside the covered school. "We are so glad to see you here, in spite of the strike and everything," said a very old one. "It really is very nice."

Trooper was restless. He tossed his head and pawed the ground. "Ride them round outside the covered school," said Angela.

"It doesn't matter how we do," said June to no one in particular. "What matters much more is Buccaneer."

"Do you think they can see us yet at home?" asked James.

"You mean on TV? No, there are no cameras outside," replied Angela. She was biting her nails, which was a bad sign.

The judges had arrived now - a short woman with straight hair, and a man with rimless glasses. A teacher in a riding mac took them inside the covered school where they could see the arena laid out, waiting for them.

"We can't possibly win," said June. "You only have to look at their horses to know."

"But what about their instructor? I bet she can't touch Angela," retorted James.

Gavin was hating both June and James. They looked small and shabby, and quite incapable of winning anything. The Witch had her ears back and when anyone passed her she made an ugly face. "We begin in five minutes. Is your team ready?" asked the teacher.

Angela nodded. "More or less."

"We'll toss to see who goes first." The Red team won.

"It's us to go first. Are you ready, Gavin? Warm him up a bit. Don't trot so fast, more collected."

He wasn't frightened. It was as though he had been waiting for this all his life. He checked his girths, and told himself to relax, keep your hands in the right place, keep calm - show them.

The judges were conferring. The gallery in the covered school was full of girls in uniform, "Packed out," Mum would have called it. Then someone announced, "The Blue team will go first." And a girl in a black coat and cream breeches, riding a brown in a double bridle, adjusted her stirrups.

"I'm first," she drawled. "Keep your fingers crossed."

"She's riding in a double bridle, so she won't get the three bonus points for use of snaffle," remarked Angela. "We are riding in the middle now."

Gavin dismounted. "I've got at least fifteen minutes to spare then," he said. "Why did they have to toss up if they were sending the other team first?" He looked round him and all he seemed to see was money speaking, as his Mum would say. It spoke on the girls' faces, in their voices, in the way they walked – money! They had always had it. And he hated them.

They couldn't see the first competitor ride, but presently she came out and the second went in. She had red hair and was called Julia, and rode a grey which carried itself like an Arab. They were only the second team, but they looked like experts.

"She's in a double bridle too. What a pity," said Angela.

"Who for?" asked June.

"Them."

The big doors were opened again and she came out saying, "I went wrong. I forgot to canter between A and F. The others will be furious." Her eyes were full of tears.

106

"I bet I do the same thing," said June.

"Same here," agreed James.

The girl rode away and the last member of the team disappeared through the doors, on a chestnut which fretted and tossed its head. "He'll never settle," Angela said. "You should beat the Blue team."

"We won't," replied James. "I know I'm going to forget the test. What happens after the halt when you stand still for four seconds? I can't remember . . ." He was shaking like a leaf. Getting lost in the test was worse than getting lost in the woods. It was like trying to remember something completely vital to your whole existence and not being able to. He could feel confusion and panic growing in his brain . . . "Proceed at ordinary trot. Turn right at B," Angela told him. "Keep calm, James." She was talking to him like a nervous horse, her hand on his shoulder. "You can do it," she said. "Just keep calm."

"I can't," he said. "I am trying, but I can't."

The girl on the chestnut had come out.

Gavin was ready now, sitting straight like a soldier, without any fear. "Ready?" asked the ancient teacher. "Are your girths tight, dear?"

"Yes, Miss," he said, "I'm ready. I've been ready a long time." He nearly added, for most of my life. But now the doors were sliding back. ENTER AT ORDINARY TROT (sitting or rising). I'll sit, he decided. Steady, Trooper, steady. They were going in now, Trooper perfectly balanced between his hands and legs, his hocks under him, his nose dropped, looking every inch a dressage horse.

"He's going very well," said Angela. "Look at him. He's like a professional. If he remembers the test he'll be the best yet."

He had halted now in the centre, was saluting, was moving off, tracking right, his body tense but calm. He had no trouble with the serpentine; he seemed to belong with Trooper, to be part of him, there was no other word for it. He was cantering now between C and M, and then circling at B. He could feel Trooper flexed round his inside leg before be changed the rein at K. Then he walked, before turning left to halt at X, to count slowly to four, still as a statue, before moving off again. There was another circle, another ordinary trot. Angela was in the gallery now. He could see her dark hair. He turned down the centre at A. He halted, saluted, felt his whole body go limp with relief, and rode out on a loose rein.

James and June waited like people waiting for the firing squad. He threw himself to the ground and started to give Trooper sugar.

"Are you ready, dear?" asked the old teacher, smiling at June.

"Yes."

"Girths tight, dear?"

"Yes."

"She's crazy about girths," Gavin said. But no one smiled. The Red team were exercising their ponies, cantering circles. Angela appeared.

"Congratulations, Gavin. That was tremendous," she said. "Your general impression was marvellous and that can mean ten more marks, though most likely you'll get about eight."

June was riding in now, her legs weak as water, the test buzzing in her head, a pain in her side, hope dwindling. Yet, when she started to ride, everything came back - her head cleared completely, her legs regained their strength and she became completely involved. Flotsam went calmly, without brilliance but with accuracy. He went into all his corners, increased his pace at the right moment and stood still when she halted for the second time. She was even beginning to enjoy herself when she reached the centre again, saluted and rode out on a loose rein, thinking over and over again, I've done it, I didn't forget.

People were clapping from the gallery. The great doors were sliding open; wintry sunshine welcomed her outside.

"Ready, dear? Are your girths tight?" It was James's turn now.

"You dare forget your test," muttered Gavin between his teeth.

"It was marvellous! I wish I was still there doing it," cried June. "I wish it could have gone on for ever. Flotsam was super, absolutely first-class. He knew the whole thing himself. He's the cleverest pony in the world."

The doors had closed behind James; there was no escaping now. He was so nervous that his whole body shook.

We haven't got enough impulsion. The Witch is half asleep, he thought, trotting towards X, and rising. His hands shook on the reins. If only the others had done badly, he thought, halting, saluting, it wouldn't matter then if I made a mistake.

The Witch nearly cut the next corner and then he had reached the serpentine, three big loops finishing at C. The Witch knew at once what was expected of her; she moved rather too fast but otherwise it was perfect and his confidence was coming back, for he had much more time to think: use your legs, James, keep contact with her mouth, don't let her run on her forehand. And then he was halting at X for the second time, counting to four very slowly, thinking, I'm half way through and I'm not forgetting the test and she's better on the other rein. And then he had come to the second serpentine and after that the circle on the left rein and the ordinary trot when he remembered to sit, and the turn down the centre which The Witch rushed rather, then the last halt of them all and the final salute ... He hadn't forgotten anything, no whistle had blown, no kind voice called, "You've gone wrong. Go back to C or A or X ..." He had done it all without one single mistake.

June was jumping up and down outside. "Did you forget it?" she cried. Angela was running round the outside of the school. "Jolly good, James," she said. "The Witch rushed a bit, but it wasn't bad at all, and we were all in snaffles so we collect three bonus marks for a start. Let's tie up the ponies and watch the Red."

Now Gavin wasn't hating them any more, not hating anyone. He was feeling relaxed and happy, almost carefree.

They took time tying up the ponies, so they were only able to see the last member of the Red team ride. She was a tall girl with long hair in a net, and a superbly cut black coat. She rode a wonderful test. "We'll never beat her," said June. "We haven't a hope. I'll never look like that, not if I live to a hundred and ride every day."

"She wasn't as good as Gavin. Trooper moved more freely," Angela replied. "And she is their best to date."

So there was still hope as they left the covered school, with the jumping to come.

110

"I wish we could miss dinner," June said, "I don't feel like eating. I've got the colly-wobbles. I bet Mum's got the television on already and I bet she's eating in front of it. She's like that, always early for everything." But she wasn't really thinking of Mum. She was thinking of the jumps going up in the covered school at this very moment. And James was thinking, I bet I lose my way on the course and get disqualified and then what will Gavin say? And Angela will be so disappointed. She won't say anything, but it will show on her face, and Mum will be disappointed too, sitting at home watching. Oh, why did I come? Why didn't I get sick this morning? If you put a finger down your throat you can make yourself sick. He wasn't frightened of the jumps, only of the responsibility of representing the school, of not letting down Angela whom he loved better than anyone else, even his own mother.

Chapter Eleven

THEY were given their lunch at a separate table in the big school dining-room. The noise was deafening. Three junior girls waited on them. They were younger than June and James and they kept giggling and pushing one another. There was meat and three vegetables, and fruit salad and ice cream. Angela opened her mail while they ate. "I didn't have time this morning," she explained.

"I'll never be able to jump Flotsam after this," announced June. Gavin ate steadily without talking; the central heating was on and he was sweating beneath his coat. There were shields of oak above a great wooden fireplace, and old school photographs, faded and brown with age.

"Gosh, one from America," remarked Angela, opening an envelope with her fingernail. "It's a long time since I heard from there. I worked there once, you know, donkeys' years ago. I rode for a dealer."

"How super," replied June, wondering if the jumps were up yet, whether they would be allowed to walk the course, how the other team had really done.

Then James shouted, "There's the minibus - and all their chairs scraped back and the whole dining-room seemed to be on its feet. Naomi and Nancy waved through the window. "We'll go round to the ponies," they shrieked.

"What about Buccaneer?" asked Angela, going to the

door.

"The vet hasn't been yet."

"How did you do?" asked Nancy.

"Quite well. I think we're neck and neck with their A team," replied Angela.

They were all outside now, standing on the paving which surrounded a fountain. Beyond was the lawn, and in the distance, the ha-ha. It's beautiful beyond words, thought Gavin. Then he saw his mother coming, waving a carrier bag, and smoking the inevitable cigarette.

"Have you had your dinner," she called. "I got 'ere after all."

"Yes." He was hurrying away already. He couldn't bear to have her invade this other life of his. He wished she hadn't come. They found Naomi and Nancy grooming the ponies and the games mistress watching.

"You can walk the course now if you like," said a tall, fair-haired girl with a badge, which said, PREFECT, on her blazer.

"Where do I go?" asked Gavin's mother, still clutching the carrier bag, through which juice from meat or tomato dripped. She wore no stockings and high-heeled shoes, and it was November! Gavin couldn't look at her. He felt ashamed.

There were ten jumps, starting with a brush and ending with three fences close together - a road-closed sign, a gate and a triple. "Those won't be easy," said Angela. "Don't cut the corner at the top, keep your nerve, let them go on a bit for the triple."

June couldn't speak now. The pain was back in her side. It seemed impossible that she would ever get round. James was looking at the telly cameras installed among the rafters in the roof. Gavin was thinking, there's nothing difficult; it's all straightforward. It's not even high for Trooper.

Naomi and Nancy had the ponies ready when they went outside again. You are second to go, Gavin," Naomi told him. "You're not going one after another in a team this time."

The gallery was full of onlookers. There were crowds of parents now. The drive was like a car park, with Rolls Royces parked alongside vans and Land Rovers. People were streaming up the drive escorted by pupils of the school.

A reporter was asking James his name. "Say it again," he said, while James shook with nerves. Then there was a flash as someone took a photograph, and the reporter moved on to June, so that she hardly saw Gavin riding in after the girl on the chestnut had come out. He pushed his crash cap more firmly on his head, trying to forget that his mother was sitting up there in the gallery among the snobs and nobs, with her old mac over last year's summer dress, because she had nothing else good enough to wear.

Trooper pranced a little. He always rose to an occasion. Gavin halted at the top, bowed a little and waited for the starting bell. When it sounded, he started Trooper on the off leg and, in less than a second, they were over the brush and approaching the Sussex gate, before turning right for the wall. Trooper shortened his stride at the last minute, changed legs behind, jumped the gate, and cantered steadily on over the wall. Now there was another turn and a hog's back made out of natural wood, with its bark still there, then cross-bars and a rail in front of a ditch, a stile, and then only the final three jumps, one after another. He turned the corner slowly, letting Trooper break into a trot, before collecting him again, sending him on, over the road-closed jump, the gate, then on towards the triple. He was nearly round; the people in the gallery were ready to clap, their hands raised, but at that moment the third bar of the triple fell, though why Gavin never knew. Afterwards Angela called it fate. But now cantering out of the ring, Gavin was filled with dismay. He had never been a good loser.

He could only control his temper with great difficulty and he felt unable to speak. He rode past everyone else without saying anything, fighting back tears of rage and disappointment. "Bad luck, Gavin," shouted June.

"It was a jolly good round," called Naomi.

"It's a very difficult course," said the prefect, smiling at him. But he replied to none of them. He dismounted, loosened Trooper's girths, and found some sugar for him in his pocket. I've let everyone down. If the others do clear rounds they'll never speak to me again. "Why did you do it, Trooper?" he asked, shaking him by his mane. "Why, why, why?"

June's turn had come. The member of the A team had just done a clear round. "I shan't do one," June said. "I'm not good enough. I can't. I don't know why you chose me, Angela."

"Wake him up, keep him going, use your legs," replied Angela. And now June was alone, just herself and Flotsam approaching the first jump, popping over it almost from a standstill, and from the gallery someone was shouting, "Use your legs, your stick, anything, wake him up." But for the next three seconds she could hardly move; she felt frozen by the responsibility she carried, unable to do anything, and as weak as cotton wool. Then she heard Angela shout, "Legs, June, legs," and suddenly she was riding as she had never ridden before, over the Sussex gate, the wall, the hog's back, the crossbars, the rail and ditch, round the flag at the top and on towards the three close together, going far too fast, but unable to do anything now but keep saying again and again, "Come on, Flotsam, you can do it, come on . ." Nothing had fallen and the clapping began.

With it came the feeling of triumph and the thought over and over again, I've done a clear round, I've beaten Gavin.

Her hands were round Flotsam's neck as she left the ring, and even the posh girls with their caps tipped over their eyes, said. "Oh, well done. Was it really clear? Jolly good. He's a sweet little pony, isn't he?"

"The best, the best in the world," said June, throwing herself to the ground, asking, "Hasn't anyone any oats for him? He was marvellous."

There was another clear round from the A team and only one left to go. Now it was James's turn. He rode in rather slowly, thinking, Mum's watching, millions are watching.

The Witch knew what was expected of her. She was a moody mare, but today was one of her good days. James let her take charge. He held onto the third plait in her mane as she jumped the brush, the wall and the frightening Sussex gate without any help from him; the hog's back and the cross-bars were easy and so was the ditch and rail, and now he expected her to take him over the rest. He sat quite still and simply turned her towards the last three. She jumped the first and the second but she wasn't right for the triple. She refused, sliding into it, while James pitched over her head into a sea of falling poles.

He was up in a moment and a steward caught The Witch. He was filled with shame as he found his stirrup and swung into the saddle again. I've let them all down, he thought, taking her back to the corner, because he had to jump all three again.

And now he used his legs as he had never used them before. The Witch shook her head, put her hocks under her, and cleared them all with inches to spare. James could hear the crowd cheering as he left and knew it was because he had mounted and gone on and finished but it didn't help. Nothing would help now he had let the side down.

"You were worse than me," Gavin said, using his posh voice. "And I was bad enough. We're definitely out of it now." He had forgotten his mother in the gallery. He could only think of his own mistakes and James's.

"Stop being beastly. You weren't so good yourself," said June.

"Exactly," said a small girl in school uniform. "And you are much the biggest too. And you've got the biggest pony."

"I wish I could see what's going on inside," exclaimed June. "The last competitor has been in there an awful long time and it's the last of the Red team."

"Perhaps she's refusing," suggested James.

"She can't be. She was the best of the lot in the dressage."

But they were all on edge now. Supposing she refused and fell off, like James? Who would win then? People said they were leading in the dressage, that Gavin's

117

dressage had been superb. They felt hope coming back as they walked up and down biting their nails.

"Penelope has an awful temper," said the small girl. "And when Mermaid refuses to jump, she refuses and that is that, if you know what I mean."

And now Penelope and Mermaid were coming out. No one was clapping, and then Angela came round the corner of the covered school to say, "She had three refusals. So we are still in the running. It all depends on how we did in the dressage. They are adding the marks together now. Are you all right, James?"

"Yes. But I'm sorry. I am really, Angela," he said.

"It doesn't matter. We all make mistakes," Angela replied. "We make them all our lives." But she wasn't really attending. She was waiting for the announcement of the winners, like everyone else, though a girl from the Blue team was still jumping.

And then at last it came: "East Hanley Comprehensive School wins by one point," and they were all cheering and reaching for their stirrups to mount. "But how did we do it?" shouted June. "I don't understand."

"One of their ponies blew up in the dressage," answered Angela. "The first one."

"Blew up?" asked Gavin.

"Started jumping about. And then two of them had double bridles. And that lost them six bonus points, which just shows one should pay attention to detail," smiled Angela.

Then they were riding in, imagining their Mums watching, and June was wishing that Fiona could have been there too, that Buccaneer could be all right. If that was so, life would be perfect, she thought.

They rode outside again, clutching their rosettes, and

then Gavin returned to collect the prize for the best individual performance.

"Your dressage was excellent," said one of the judges, tying the rosette to Trooper's bridle. "I do hope you'll keep up your riding. I think you have a great future."

The words hit him like the impact of a sledgehammer, for where was he going from here? To a butcher's shop, or to the building site, but not to ride any more. This would be his first and his last great success - unless a miracle should happen, and that wasn't likely, not to someone like himself. So he rode round the covered riding school without smiling, while his mother called, "Well done, Gavin," wanting everyone to know that he was her son.

After that there was tea in the big dining-room, with iced cakes and neatly-cut sandwiches, while the sky darkened outside. The judges kept praising the teams. "You were marvellous," they told James. "You rode with such guts after your fall."

And then it was time to go home, flushed with triumph. But before that happened the girls of the school rose to their feet to sing, "For they are jolly good fellows, and so say all of us," and then to roar three cheers for the winning team: "Hip, hip, hooray!"

They were almost drunk with triumph by this time; only Buccaneer's illness stood between them and a feeling of total happiness. They went round shaking hands, expressing their thanks, and Angela made a short speech. The ponies were ready in the horsebox, when they returned to the yard.

Girls called, "Goodbye," through the gathering darkness. There were lights on in all the buildings. The girls who had ridden were rugging up their ponies.

"What a day," exclaimed Angela. "You don't get many like this in your lifetime." She climbed into the cab with Gavin. A teacher said, "Come again next year and we'll beat you," and slammed the door shut.

June and James settled themselves in the groom's compartment. The horsebox rumbled away down the drive until the lights of the school were like fairy lights in the distance.

"We won, we won, do you realise it?" cried James, pinching himself to make sure he wasn't dreaming. "There will be a cup in the school with our names on it."

"Yes," replied June, thinking of Buccaneer and Fiona waiting alone for the vet, of the vet injecting something into Buccaneer's neck, or feeding him intravenously, or at the worst Buccaneer dying. If only Gavin had controlled his temper everything would be perfect now, she thought.

The rosettes were up in the cab - four reds. The driver and Angela talked until presently the driver turned to Gavin and said, "What are you going to do when you leave school, son? You rode so well today, it would be a pity to give it up."

Gavin looked out into the darkness. "I don't know," he answered.

"Work with horses?"

"Not enough money."

"You'd be too young to drive one of these, or I'd take you on," said the driver.

"I've got a suggestion," said Angela. "Just wait till I get something out of my trouser pocket."

Chapter Twelve

SHE pulled out a letter. "Would you like to go to the United States?" she asked.

Gavin waited for the driver to speak. "You don't mean me?" he asked after a time. "Aren't I too young and what would Mum say?" But even as he spoke he was seeing skyscrapers, Cadillacs, Coca-Cola in tall glasses, the wildness and the richness which he thought was America.

"It's an old buddy of mine," Angela exclaimed. "He's written to me, and I thought you might be interested. He writes like this: *Do you by any chance know of a boy or a girl who would come out here and ride for me? (I guess a boy would be swell because they don't need too much looking after). I could offer him or her two hundred dollars a month plus full board. I would train them real good, and they could do the circuit come the autumn if they make out all right. I'll see they get their visa and tell the authorities. I need someone real bad. I do hope you can help . . . etc, etc,"* finished Angela, folding up the letter, while the driver said, "That's good money, that must be sixty pounds a month near enough."

Enough to pay my mother seven pounds a week, thought Gavin, even to pay Fiona compensation if Buccaneer never gets better. And I'll get away from the rubbish dump. I'll be free, and I'll still be riding. I won't have to give it up.

"The answer," said Gavin, in his special posh voice, is "Yes, a thousand times yes."

"It's a long way from here," said Angela. "You must realise that. It can be lonely. Americans don't really speak our language, you think they do, but they don't. And it's a big country. I don't think people are so tolerant as here. If you let horses out on purpose there, they won't give you a second chance, no siree. You will be on the first boat back to Britain."

"So you know!" exclaimed Gavin. "Why didn't you say anything, Miss?"

"I wanted us to win today. You were the best. And making a scene, upsetting you, would hardly have helped Buccaneer."

He wanted to say, "I'm sorry. I feel awful about it." But it sounded babyish, and after all he was nearly fifteen.

"I'll write and tell him about you. You'll have to go through immigration. They'll take your fingerprints when you go to the Embassy. They'll vet you like a horse, and delve into your background and character. It can be humiliating, but don't get on your high horse. Suffer in silence and with luck you'll be on your way in the spring. By the autumn you'll be doing the circuit. You can be my working pupil in the holidays and I'll polish up your jumping."

"What's the circuit?" he asked.

"A round of shows which lasts right through the autumn, ending I believe in Madison Square Gardens and taking in Toronto."

He saw himself jumping in stadium after stadium, the lights shining on him, the crowds cheering. "I don't deserve it. And I don't know how to thank you, Miss."

"Well, don't then, and for the millionth time, not Miss. Look, we're home," cried Angela.

Fiona was waiting in the yard. "What luck?" she shouted. "You didn't win, did you?"

"Yes," shouted June and James, half falling out of the horsebox. "We won by a point, and Gavin's won the individual! We had a super time. I wish you could have been there," shouted June. "How's Buccaneer? I've been thinking about him all the time."

"He's all right," replied Fiona. "He's out of danger, But he has laminitis - it goes with the illness, but he's going to be all right." She looked very tired, like some-one who had been worrying for a long time, though she knew that tonight she would sleep and that the night-mare was over.

Naomi and Nancy were leading the ponies down the ramp.

"Come and look at him," said Fiona, and the four of them stood gazing at Buccaneer over the loose box door.

"I want to apologise for what I did," said Gavin. It was really the first time he had said he was sorry since he had been taken from the Hopkins' farm all those years ago. He felt freer when he had said it. But Fiona couldn't answer, for she was still hating him for all the agony and misery he had caused. She couldn't forgive him, not yet. "I've got to go now," she said without look-ing at Gavin. "I'm returning to school tonight. But I'll be ringing you every evening, Angela to check on Buc-caneer. I'm so glad you won."

She hated leaving Buccaneer. "His powders are in the tack room," she called. "He is to have two a day, and some exercise if you can manage it."

She was running now, for she had stayed too long

waiting for them to come home, and she found her mother waiting in the hall. "We must leave at once," she cried. "I've packed. I just hope I've put everything in."

"He's out of danger. He's going to be all right," shrieked Fiona, "And they won."

June put an arm round Flotsam. "You are marvellous," she said. "Sleep well. I'll see you tomorrow." The road home was dark, but it didn't matter. Nothing mattered beside the fact that Buccaneer was all right, even their victory was nothing compared to it. She started to run. Mum was waiting to open the back door.

"You were smashing," she cried. "I'm so chuffed. I can't stop crying."

"And Buccaneer's all right," June said. "Are you listening, Mum? Buccaneer's all right."

James's mother put her arms round his neck, "You were great," she said. "Real great. And how you got on and rode again I shall never know. It was so plucky. Oh Jamie, I'm so proud of you. You don't know how proud."

"And Buccaneer's well again," James said. "That's what really matters."

Suddenly he started to dance round the small kitchen. "Everything's all right," he cried. "I didn't let them down. I didn't. One of the girls did worse. She had three refusals. The Witch was marvellous, and I really know how to jump now. Oh, it was wonderful, Mum. And they all sang that we were jolly good fellows, and cheered us. It was as good as a football match."

The rest of the family had gathered round him now. And some children were knocking at the door and calling, "Is James back? We saw him on telly."

His happiness knew no bounds. "It was the best day of my life," he said.

"And it isn't over yet. We're going to have a celebration," announced Mum.

Gavin was home now.

"You didn't speak to me, not once, Gavin," his Mum said. "There I was waving like mad and you didn't so much as turn your head."

He didn't say anything, except, "I'm going to America in the spring, Mum. I'm going to send you seven pounds a week in lovely, lovely dollars, and you won't even have to feed me out of it. And when I get a rise I'll send you more and you'll be able to get that little house you're always dreaming about on a mortgage. Angela's fixing it up. I'm going in the spring."

He had been thinking about it all the way home. It was happiness at the end of a long road of frustration. He had thought he would never escape, that he would always be with the rubbish dump and the endless shortage of money. It was as good as winning the football pools.

"You're dreaming," his Mum said. "Or joking."

"I'm not, go and ring up Angela if you don't believe me, go on." He could hardly believe it himself. He knew he didn't deserve such luck, and vowed he would never let Angela or anyone else down again.

"I'm going to ride horses for an American," he said. "I'm going to do the circuit. Soon I shall go to the American Embassy in Grosvenor Square and be vetted and interviewed. And when I've made my fortune I shall come home and buy a farm with lots of fruit trees." And he thought, it all began there with the Hopkins and the old grey mare and the apple trees. The last few years have just been an interlude; now I'm back where I was. I'm going to ride all the time. It's going to be my life and no one can change it, not even Mum. And looking at her tired face, he felt the grudge which he had held against her all these years ebb away.

"And I will come and see you," she cried. "Where are the boys? We must tell them, they'll be so excited. Perhaps you'll be able to fix them up with jobs too when the time comes."

His brothers came in, their faces covered with dirt "We saw you on telly. The whole school did. You should have seen the old head, he was cheering like mad, standing up and shouting, 'Go on, ride, ride, will you?' It was smashing."

"I'm going to the United States," Gavin told them. He saw himself riding into a golden sunset on a grey horse.

"We expected you back three days ago," Matron said. "What *have* you been doing? Your bed has been changed; you're sleeping next to the door. Now don't pull a face."

"I'm not. I mean I didn't mean to. I don't mind any more about where I sleep." And it was true. Petty things like that would never matter in the same way again, not after the last few days, not now that Buccaneer was supposed to be all right. But Fiona was still afraid, so she put her case just inside the dormitory door and ran downstairs to the call box in the hall to telephone Angela.

"Is Buccaneer all right?" she asked when she was through.

"Oh hullo, it's Fiona," said Angela. "He's fine. Almost his old self. So stop worrying. You'll be riding him again when you're home for half term."

"You really think so?"

"Yes."

She put the receiver down and went back upstairs. Only eight days to half term, she thought. I shan't ride him far. I shall only walk. And she saw him getting fitter, and though the twenty-mile ride would be too much for him, there would be other things. Girls were coming back from supper. They charged into the dormitory shouting, "So you're back. You were away a heck of a time. Matron was in a lovely old tizzy."

She took a photograph of Buccaneer out of her case and put it on her chest of drawers. "I couldn't come back. He nearly died," she said. "He ate ragwort. Usually they die, but he had the best vet in England." But now it was more like relating a dream than what had really happened, for the most frightening moments were fading already, softened by time. "And the local Comprehensive beat Sundean Girls."

"They didn't, not really? Gosh."

"Yes. It's a long story. I think I'm going to bed. I haven't really slept for days," Fiona said. The bed was newly made. The owls hooted in the trees in the garden. People talked incessantly. Matron came in and out complaining, but Fiona slept through it all, dreaming of herself riding round Badminton Horse Trials on Buccaneer.